JACKIE COLLINS

Hey Readers,

   Welcome to "The Bitch" — The new REVISED VERSION! I started to Read it through one day, and I thought about all the little changes I would like to make. So I did! I do hope you enjoy this latest version of a book I wrote as an original paperback quite a few years ago.   I have to say that I still love the characters, and "The Bitch" is a fun book — a lot better than the movie!

   Happy Reading —

   Jackie C.

Praise for Jackie Collins

'Sex, power and intrigue – no one does it better than Jackie.' *heat*

'A tantalising novel packed with power struggles, greed and sex. This is Collins at her finest. *****' *Closer*

'Bold, brash, whiplash fast – with a cast of venal rich kids, this is classic Jackie Collins' *Marie Claire*

'Sex, money, power, murder, betrayal, true love – it's all here in vintage Collins style. Collins's plots are always a fabulously involved, intricate affair, and this docs not disappoint.' *Daily Mail*

'Her style is pure escapism, her heroine's strong and ambitious and her men, well, like the book, they'll keep you up all night!' *Company*

'A generation of women have learnt more about how to handle their men from Jackie's books than from any kind of manual . . . Jackie is very much her own person: a total one off' *Daily Mail*

'Jackie is still the queen of sexy stories. Perfect' *OK!*

'Cancel all engagements, take the phone off the hook and indulge yourself' *Mirror*

Also by Jackie Collins

The Power Trip
Married Lovers
Lovers & Players
Deadly Embrace
Hollywood Wives – The New Generation
Lethal Seduction
Thrill!
L.A. Connections – Power, Obsession, Murder, Revenge
Hollywood Kids
American Star
Rock Star
Hollywood Husbands
Lovers & Gamblers
Hollywood Wives
The World Is Full Of Divorced Women
The Love Killers
Sinners
The Stud
The World Is Full Of Married Men
Hollywood Divorces

THE SANTANGELO NOVELS

Goddess of Vengeance
Poor Little Bitch Girl
Drop Dead Beautiful
Dangerous Kiss
Vendetta: Lucky's Revenge
Lady Boss
Lucky
Chances

Jackie Collins

THE
BITCH

**SIMON &
SCHUSTER**

London · New York · Sydney · Toronto · New Delhi

A CBS COMPANY

First published in Great Britain by Pan Books, 1979.

This revised edition published by Simon & Schuster UK Ltd, 2012
A CBS COMPANY

1 3 5 7 9 10 8 6 4 2

Simon & Schuster UK Ltd
1st Floor
222 Gray's Inn Road
London WC1X 8HB

Simon & Schuster Australia, Sydney
Simon & Schuster India, New Delhi

www.simonandschuster.co.uk

A CIP catalogue record for this book is available from the British Library

ISBN 978-1-84983-648-7

Typeset by Hewer Text UK Ltd, Edinburgh
Printed and bound in Great Britain by CPI Group (UK) Ltd,
Croydon, CR0 4YY

For
J. K.

Chapter One

Nico Constantine rose from the blackjack table, smiled all round, threw the pretty croupier a large tip, and pocketed twelve gold five-hundred-dollar chips. A nice six-thousand dollars. Not bad for a fast half hour's work. Not good for someone who was already down two hundred thousand.

Nico surveyed the crowded Las Vegas casino. His intense dark eyes flicked back and forth amongst the assembled company. Little old ladies in floral dresses exhibited surprising strength as their skinny arms pulled firmly on the slot machines. Florid faced couples – weak with excitement and too much sun – picked up a fast eighty- or ninety-dollars at the roulette tables. Strolling hookers – blank eyes alert for the big spenders. The big spenders themselves, in

1

polyester leisure suits, screeched away in middle-American accents at the crap tables.

Nico smiled. Las Vegas always amused him. The hustle and the bustle. The win and the lose. The total fantasy of it all.

Vegas was a carousel town set in the middle of arid desert. A blazing array of neon signs housing all the vices known to man. And a few unknown ones. In Vegas, if you could pay for it, you could get it. Just name it.

He lit a long narrow Havana cigar with a wafer-thin gold Dunhill lighter, smiled again and nodded at the people who went out of their way to catch his eye. A pit boss here, a cigarette girl there, a security guard on his rounds. Nico Constantine was a well-known man in Vegas. More importantly Nico Constantine was a gentleman – and how many of those were there left in the world?

He looked good. For forty-nine years of age he looked exceptionally good. A full head of black hair – curly, with slight traces of grey that only enhanced the jet. Dark eyes – unfairly surrounded with thick black lashes. A strong nose. Olive skin beautifully tanned. A wide-shouldered, thin-hipped body that would make many a younger man envious.

However, the most attractive thing about Nico was his style, his aura, his charisma.

Hand-finished, tailor-made three-piece suits in the

very finest cloth. Silk shirts of exquisite quality. Italian-made shoes in glove-soft leather. Nothing but the best for Nico Constantine. It had been his motto since he was twenty years of age.

'Can I get you a drink, Mr Constantine?' A cocktail waitress was at his side, long legs in sexy cobweb stockings, a wide mouth smiling and full of Vegas promise.

He smiled back at her. Naturally he had wonderful teeth, and all his own, with just one vagabond gypsy cap. 'Why not? I think vodka, on the rocks.' His dark eyes flirted with her outrageously, and she loved every minute of it. Women always did. Women positively adored Nico Constantine and he, in his turn, was certainly not averse to them. From a cocktail waitress, to a princess, he treated them all the same. Flowers (always red roses); champagne (always Cristal); presents (small gold charms from Tiffany in New York, or, if they lasted more than a few weeks, little diamond trinkets from Cartier).

The cocktail waitress went off to get his drink.

Nico consulted his Patek Phillipe digital gold watch. It was eight o'clock. The evening was ahead of him. He would sip his drink, watch the action, then he would step once more into the fray, and fate would decide his future.

* * *

Nico Constantine was born in a poor suburb of Athens. He was the first brother to three sisters, and his childhood had been that of a small boy caught up in a sea of femininity. His sisters fussed, bullied and smothered him. His mother spoiled him and various female relatives kissed, cuddled and catered to him at all times.

His father was away a lot, being a crewman on one of the fabulous Onassis yachts, so Nico became the little man of the family. He was a beautiful baby, a cute little toddler, a devastating young boy and by the time he left school at fourteen, every female in the vicinity loved him madly.

His three sisters, not to forget his mother, guarded him ferociously. To them he was a prince.

When his father decided to take him away on a trip as a cabin boy, the entire family rebelled. No way was Nico to be allowed out of their sight. Absolutely no way. His poor father argued, but to no avail, and Nico was given a job in a nearby fishing port on the small dock not a hundred yards from where one of his sisters worked scraping fish. She watched him like a hawk. If he so much as talked to a member of the female sex she would appear, bossy and predatory.

The Constantine family went out of their way to keep young Nico as innocent and untouched as possible. They worked on it as a team.

Nico meanwhile was growing up. His body was

developing, his balls were dropping, his penis was growing, and most of the time he felt as horny as hell. Well who wouldn't, living in close proximity to four women? His sexual senses were assailed on every level. Naked breasts. Body hair. Tempting female smells. Underclothes hanging up to dry every way he turned.

By the time he was sixteen he was desperate. To jerk off was his only relief, but even that had to be planned like a military operation. Female eyes watched him constantly.

He realized he must run away, although it was a difficult decision to make, leaving behind all that love and adoration. It had to be done though. He was being smothered. It was the only answer, the only way he could become a real man.

He left on a Sunday night in December, arriving in the city of Athens two days later, cold, tired, hungry, certain he had made a wrong move, and already anxious that his family would come chasing after him. He had no idea what to do, how to get a job, or even what kind of job to look for. He wandered around the city, freezing in his thin cotton trousers and shirt, with only an oilskin to keep out the biting ice and sleet.

Finally he took shelter in the entrance of a tall apartment building, and stayed there until a chauffeured car pulled up, and two women in furs got out, chattering and laughing together.

Instinct told him to attract their attention. He coughed loudly, caught the eye of one of the women, smiled appealingly and winked, projecting unthreatening vulnerability.

'Yes?' the woman asked. 'Do you want my autograph?'

He was always quick, and without hesitation said, 'I have travelled three days to get your autograph.'

He had no idea who she was, only that she was mysteriously beautiful, with soft pale curls, a slender figure beneath the open fur, and a sympathetic smile.

She walked over to him and he inhaled sweet perfume. It reminded him of the womanly smells of home.

'You look exhausted,' she said. Her voice was magical, vibrant and comforting.

Nico didn't answer. He just looked at her with his dark eyes until she took him by the arm and said, 'Come, you shall have a hot drink and some warm clothes.'

Her name was Lise Maria Androtti. She was a very famous opera singer, thirty-three years old, divorced, extremely rich, and the most wonderful person Nico had ever met.

Within days they were lovers. The seventeen-year-old boy, and the thirty-three-year-old woman. She taught him to love her exactly as she had always wanted. And he was a willing learner. Listening, practising, achieving.

'God, Nico!' she would exclaim in the throes of ecstasy. 'You are the cleverest lover I have ever had.' And of course, after her expert tuition – he was.

Her friends were scandalized, and warnings abounded. 'He's hardly more than a child.' 'There'll be an outcry!' 'Your public will never stand for it!'

Lise Maria smiled in the face of their objections. 'He makes me happy,' she explained. 'This boy is the best thing that ever happened to me.'

Nico wrote a short formal note to his family. He was fine. He had a job. He would write again soon. He enclosed some of Lise Maria's money. She had insisted; and every month she made sure he did the same again. She understood how painful losing Nico must have been to them. He was truly a wonderful boy.

On Nico's twentieth birthday they were married. A ceremony Lise Maria tried to keep private, but every photographer in Greece turned up, and the small ceremony became a mad circus. The result was that Nico's family finally found out where their precious boy was, and they rushed to Athens, and added to the scandal Lise Maria had tried so calmly to ignore.

There was nothing they could do, it was too late. Besides which, Nico and Lise Maria seemed so unbelievably happy together.

For nineteen years they remained locked in a state of bliss, their age difference seeming to bother neither of them. Only the world press made much of it.

Nico grew from a gauche young male, into a sophisticated man of the world. He developed a taste for the very best in everything, and Lise Maria was well able to afford the millionaire lifestyle they adopted together. He never bothered to work, Lise Maria didn't want him to. He travelled everywhere with her, and taught himself fluent English, French, German and Italian.

He dabbled on the world stock market, and occasionally did well.

He learned to snow ski, water ski, drive a racing car, ride horses, play polo.

He became an expert at bridge, backgammon and poker.

He acquired an excellent knowledge of wine and cuisine.

He was a faithful and ever expanding lover to his beautiful, famous wife. He treated her like a queen right up until the day she died of cancer aged fifty-five.

Then he was lost. Set adrift in a world he did not wish to live in without his beloved Lise Maria.

He was thirty-nine years old and alone for the first time in his life. He had everything, for Lise Maria had bequeathed him her fortune. But as far as he was concerned, he had nothing. He could no longer stand to be at their Athens penthouse, their island retreat, their smart Paris house.

He sold everything. The four cars. The fabulous jewellery. The homes.

He said goodbye to his family, now ensconced in a house in the centre of Athens, and he set off for America – the one place Lise Maria had never been accepted as the superstar she was all over Europe.

America. A place to forget about his past. Onto new beginnings.

* * *

'Here's your vodka, Mr Constantine,' the cocktail waitress said, meeting his eyes with a bold glance, then reluctantly retreating at a signal from a surly pit boss.

Las Vegas. A truly unique place. Twenty-four-hour nonstop gambling. Lavish hotels and entertainment. Beautiful showgirls. Blazing sunshine.

Nico remembered with a smile his first sight of the place. Driving from Los Angeles in the dead of night, and after hours of blackness suddenly hitting this neon-lit fantasy in the middle of nowhere. It was a memory that would always linger.

Was it only ten years ago? It seemed like forever . . .

* * *

Nico had arrived in Los Angeles in the summer with twenty-five pieces of impeccable Gucci luggage. He had rented a white Mercedes, taken up residence in a bungalow attached to the famed Beverly Hills Hotel, and sat back to see if he liked it.

He liked it. Who wouldn't in his position?

He was rich, handsome, available.

He was jumped on within two minutes of settling himself in a private cabana beside the pool.

The jumpee was Dorothy Dainty, a sometime starlet with a mass of red hair, thirty-eight-inch silicone tits, and an unfortunate habit of talking out of the corner of her mouth like a refugee from a gangster movie. 'You a producer?' she asked conspiratorially.

Nico looked her over, treated her with respect, and allowed her to show him the town.

To her annoyance he didn't try to fuck her. Dorothy Dainty was amazed. Everyone tried to fuck her. Everyone succeeded. What was with this strange foreign guy?

She took him to all the best places. One visit and Nico and the maître d' were the best of friends. After two weeks he didn't need Dorothy. He sent her a gold charm inscribed with a few kind words, a dozen red roses, and he never called her again.

'The guy has to be gay!' Dorothy told all her friends. 'Has to be!'

The thought of a man who didn't actually want to fuck her threw her into a decline for weeks. It took her a while to recover.

Nico had no intention of screwing the Dorothy Dainty's of this world. His wife had been dead three months, and he certainly felt the physical need of a woman, but nothing would make him lower his standards. He'd had the best, and while he accepted the fact that he would never find another Lise Maria, he was certainly looking for something better than Dorothy Dainty.

He decided young girls would be best for him. Fresh-faced beauties with no track record.

He had never been to bed with a woman other than his wife. During the next ten years he made up for lost time and made love to one-hundred-and-twenty fresh-faced beauties. They lasted on an average four weeks each, and not one of them ever regretted having been made love to by Nico Constantine. He was an ace lover. The very best.

He bought himself a mansion in the Hollywood hills, and settled down to having a good time.

The bachelors of the Beverly Hills community flocked around to be his friend. He had everything they all wanted. Class. Style. Panache. The money wasn't so impressive, they all had money, but he had that indefinable quality – a charm that was inborn.

For ten idyllic years Nico lived the good life. He played tennis, swam, worked the stock market, gambled with his friends, invested in the occasional deal, made love to beautiful girls, sunbathed, saunaed, went to the best parties, movies and restaurants.

It was a grave shock to him when his money finally ran out.

Nico Constantine broke. Ridiculous. But true. His late wife's lawyers in Athens had been warning him for two years that the estate was running dry. They had wanted him to invest, diversify his capital. Nico had taken no notice, until eventually he'd spent everything there was. The thought of having no money appalled him. He decided something must be done immediately. He was a brilliant gambler, always had been, and the lure of Las Vegas was so very close.

He thought about his situation carefully. How much money did he need to maintain his present lifestyle? He supported his entire family in Athens, but apart from them there was only himself to think about. If he sold his mansion, and rented instead, he would have a substantial lump sum of money and cut his weekly expenditure immediately. It seemed like a sensible idea. He could take the money from the sale of his house, and in Vegas – with his luck and skill – he would double it – treble it – certainly build it into a substantial stake that he could invest and then live off the income.

Nico had been in Las Vegas exactly twenty-three hours. Already he was down one-hundred-and-ninety-four-thousand dollars.

Chapter Two

Fontaine Khaled awoke alone in her New York apartment. She removed her black lace sleep-mask, and reached for the orange juice in her bedside fridge.

Gulping the deliciously cold glass of liquid she groaned aloud. A mammoth hangover was threatening to engulf her entirely. Christ! Last night clubbing. Two gay studs. One black. One white. What an entertainment!

She attempted to step out of bed, but felt too weak, and collapsed back amongst her Porthault pillows.

Reaching over to her bedside table she picked up a large packet of vitamin pills, which she then washed down with orange juice.

Fontaine sighed, and stretched for a silver hand-mirror. She sat up in bed and studied her face. Yes, she still looked incredible – in spite of the terrible year she had suffered through.

Mrs Fontaine Khaled. Ex-wife of *the* Benjamin Al Khaled – multi-billionaire Arab businessman. Actually Fontaine could describe him very accurately as an Arab Shit. I mean, what kind of man got away with saying to his wife 'I divorce thee' three times, and then walked away totally and utterly free?

An Arab Shit, that's what kind of man.

Fontaine conveniently blanked out on the more gory details of why Benjamin had divorced her. He had compromised her with sneak photographs of her and a variety of young men making love. It hadn't been fair. She was entitled to lovers. Benjamin – in his sixties – was hardly likely to satisfy her most demanding needs.

The divorce still upset Fontaine and was one of the reasons she had spent the better part of the year in New York, rather than London, where everyone knew about the scandal. It wasn't Benjamin she missed so much, it was the respect and security of being Mrs Benjamin Al Khaled.

Of course she still was Mrs Khaled, but she made up a neat set of two with his other ex-wife – the one he had left to marry her. Now there was a new Mrs Khaled Mark Three. A disgustingly young model by the name of Delores. A tacky-looking girl, who was making a complete fool of Benjamin and spending all his money even faster than she had!

To Fontaine's way of thinking the divorce settlement was not equitable to her needs. Her standard of living had taken a sharp dive. She was even reduced to wearing last year's sable coat. Last year's! *Quelle* horror!

She climbed out of bed, naked as usual. A fine body, full of muscle tone and drenched in skin lotion. Firm skin, small breasts as high as a sixteen-year-old. Fontaine had always looked after herself. Massage. Steam baths. Facials. Exercises. Head-to-toe conditioning. The work she had put in had paid off. Soon she would be forty years old, and she didn't look a day over twenty-nine. No face lifts either. Just classical English beauty and good bones.

She put on a silk housecoat and rang for her maid, a plump Puerto Rican girl she was thinking of firing if only help wasn't so difficult to find these days.

The girl walked into the room without knocking. 'I wish you'd knock, Ria,' Fontaine said irritably. 'I've told you a million and one times.'

Ria smirked at her reflection in the mirrored bedroom. Oh Jeeze – would she like to fuck her boyfriend, Martino, in these surroundings!

'Sure Mrs K.,' she said casually picking at her nail polish. 'You want I should run you a bath?'

'Yes,' replied Fontaine shortly. She really couldn't stand the girl.

* * *

Sarah Grant, Fontaine's closest friend in New York, waited patiently at the Four Seasons for Fontaine to turn up for lunch. She consulted her neat Cartier Tank watch and sighed with annoyance. Fontaine was always late, one of her less endearing habits.

Sarah signalled to the waiter to bring her another martini. She was an extremely striking-looking woman, with intense Slavic features, and jet-black hair starkly rolled into a bun. She was rich in her own right, having been through two millionaire husbands, and was now married to a writer called Allan who joined in her tastes for rather bizarre sex. At the moment they were both enjoying an affair with a New England transvestite who wanted to become a folk singer.

Fontaine made her entrance. Heads still turned.

The two women kissed, mouths barely brushing each other's cheeks.

'How was Beverly Hills?' Fontaine demanded. 'Did you have a divine time?'

Sarah shrugged, 'You know how I feel about L.A. Boring and hot. Allan enjoyed it though, someone has finally been fool enough to option his screenplay.

They paid him a pittance. You would think he had personally discovered gold!'

'How sweet.'

'Adorable. My man has money at last. It will just about cover one quarter's payment on my jewellery insurance.'

Fontaine laughed. 'Sarah, you're so mean, the poor man has balls, you know.'

'Oh yes? *Do* tell me where he keeps them. I'd simply love to know.'

Lunch passed by in a flurry of the latest gossip; both women were experts. By the time coffee arrived they had carved up everyone and anyone, and enjoyed every minute of it.

Sarah sipped a liqueur. 'I saw an old friend of yours in L.A.,' she said casually. 'Remember Tony?'

'Tony?' Fontaine feigned ignorance, although she knew instantly who Sarah was talking about. Tony Blake. Tony the stud.

'He remembers you,' Sarah teased. 'And with a quite violent lack of affection. What on earth did you do to him?'

Fontaine frowned. 'I took him from being a nothing little waiter, and built him into the best manager of the best club in London.'

'Ah, I remember. Then you threw him out, didn't you?'

'I dispensed with his services before he dispensed

with minc,' Fontaine said irritably. 'The cocky little bastard was trying to open up his own place.'

Sarah laughed. 'So what happened?'

'I thought I told you all about it. I went part-ners with his money man before he could. Poetic justice. I haven't heard from him since. What's he doing in L.A.?'

'Sniffing, snorting, what everyone does in L.A. By the way, whatever happened to your club, Hobo?'

Fontaine extracted an art deco compact from her Vuitton purse and studied her face. 'My club is still going strong, still the place.' She selected a small tube of lip gloss and smoothed it over her lips with her finger. 'As a matter of fact I had a letter from my lawyer this morning. He seems to feel I should be getting back to London to sort out my affairs.'

'And what affairs are those?' Sarah asked lightly.

Fontaine snapped her compact shut. 'The mone-tary kind, darling. They're the only kind that matter, aren't they?'

* * *

After the lunch they parted and went their separate ways. Fontaine felt that she had to keep up a certain front, even with a close friend like Sarah. As she strolled along Fifth Avenue she thought about the letter from her lawyer and what it had really said.

Financial difficulties, unpaid bills, spending too much money, Hobo in trouble.

Yes, the time had come to return to London and sort things out.

But how could Hobo possibly be in trouble? From the moment Benjamin had bought the place for her it had made money. Tony, her manager, lover and stud, had become the most wanted man in London when she had put him in charge. And when she'd gotten rid of him Ian Thaine, her new partner, had redecorated the place, put in a new manager, and then got pissed off because she was not prepared to extend the partnership to a personal level. So she had bought him out, and when she left London Hobo had been flourishing. And it was all hers, and should be a substantial asset; not a goddamn drain on her finances.

It was starting to rain, and Fontaine looked around in vain for a cab. God! It was about time she found herself another millionaire. Who needed this searching for cabs garbage? She should have a chauffeur-driven Rolls as she'd always had when she was Mrs Benjamin Khaled. As it was she could only afford to hire a limousine and chauffeur for the evenings. She needed it desperately as the escorts she chose barely owned more than a motorbike – if that. Fontaine liked the men in her life to keep their assets on show – right up front – in their pants.

She had never really pursued money. Because of her devastating beauty it had always managed to pursue her. Benjamin Al Khaled had spotted her when she was modelling in a St Moritz fashion show and had dumped his first wife quicker than a hooker gives head.

After life with Benjamin, money was a necessity. Fontaine had a taste for the best that was very hard to quench.

However, she had decided to pause before searching out another billionaire husband. Billionaire equalled old (unless you counted the freaked-out rock stars who always seemed to tie themselves up with young blonde starlets). And old was not what Fontaine needed. She needed youth – she enjoyed youth – she revelled in the male body beautiful, and an eight- or nine-inch solid cock.

A drunk weaved across Fifth Avenue and planted himself, swaying and dribbling, in front of her, blocking her path. 'Ya wanna get laid?' he demanded, displaying a mouthful of leer.

Fontaine ignored him and attempted to pass.

'Hey,' he managed to obstruct her way. 'Wassamatter? You don' wanna fuck?'

Fontaine gave him a hard shove, saw a cab, ran for it, collapsed on the back seat and sighed.

It really was time to get out of New York.

* * *

The very moment Fontaine departed for her lunch date, Ria, her Puerto Rican maid, rushed to the phone. Ten minutes later her boyfriend arrived, Martino, the best-looking black guy in the whole of fuckin' New York City.

'Whatcha say, babe?' He greeted her with a kiss and a grope of her ass, while his stoned eyes checked out every inch of the luxurious apartment.

'We got two hours,' Ria said quickly. 'The bitch won't be back before that.'

'Let's go then, babe, let's get to it.'

'Sure, hon. Only thing is, well, I got me a fantasy. Can we waste five whole minutes? Can I show you her bedroom? Can we make it all over her crazy fuckin' bed?'

Martino grinned. He was already unzipping his baggy pants.

* * *

Fontaine spent the afternoon at the beauty salon listening to more gossip. Some of it was a repeat of what Sarah had already told her, but it was interesting to have it confirmed.

'I'm going back to London,' Fontaine confided to Leslie, her hairdresser.

'Yeah?' Leslie grinned. He had nice teeth, a good face, a firm body, but he was minus where he should be plus, a fact that Fontaine had personally checked.

'It's about time I had a change of scenery,' Fontaine continued. 'I feel as though I'm getting too static here.'

'I know what you mean,' Leslie replied sympathetically. Ha! Fontaine Khaled getting static! That was a laugh. The old bitch must have screwed everything under twenty-five that walked in New York City!

Leslie himself was twenty-six, and not pleased that the notorious Mrs Khaled had taken him to bed only once, and then abandoned him like a bad smell. Oh, he was still all right to do her hair – and why not – he was the best goddamn hairdresser in town. The most fashionable too.

'Will you miss me, Leslie?' Fontaine fixed him with her lethal kaleidoscope eyes.

She was flirting and Leslie knew it. *What's the matter, Mrs Khaled? Got a few hours to kill?*

'Of course I'll miss you, every time I set a wig I'll remember you!'

Game set and match to Leslie. For a change.

* * *

Fontaine was not in a good humour when she returned to her apartment. The horrible man in the street. Leslie getting smart ass. And then a foul-smelling cab driver who insisted on talking. Asshole! And she had a headache too.

Going up in the elevator she didn't bother to search for her key. She rang the doorbell, and cursed when it took Ria forever to answer.

It finally occurred to her that the stupid girl wasn't going to come to the door at all. She was probably asleep, slouched over a soap opera on television.

Furious, Fontaine rifled through her bag for her keys, found them, and let herself into the apartment with an angry commanding shout of – 'Ria! Where the hell are you!'

The sight that greeted her eyes was not a pretty one. Her apartment had been stripped, and from what she could see at first glance, what was left had been wrecked.

Shocked, she took two steps inside then, realizing that Ria might be lying mutilated and murdered amongst the debris or even that the robbers might still be on the premises, she quickly backed out.

* * *

It took the cops an hour and a half to arrive, and they discovered no murdered Ria, just 'Flocking Beech!' scrawled in lipstick all over the mirrored bedroom.

Fontaine recognized the scrawl as being Rica's illiterate scribble.

Everything that could be moved was gone. Her clothes, luggage, toiletries, sheets, towels, small items of furniture – even light fitments and all electrical gadgets including the vacuum that Ria had pushed so disdainfully around the apartment.

The bed, stripped of everything except the mattress, bore its own personal message – a congealing mass of sperm.

'God Almighty!' Fontaine exclaimed, fuming. She glared at the two patrolmen. 'Where the hell's the detective that is going to investigate this case? I have very important friends you know, and I want some action – fast!'

The two cops exchanged glances. *Let's hope to Christ they don't put Slamish on this case*, they both thought at the same time. But they knew it was inevitable. Slamish and Fontaine were destined to meet.

* * *

Chief Detective Marvin H. Slamish had three unfortunate things going for him. One – an uncontrollable defect in his left eye that caused him to wink at the most inopportune moments. Two – a tendency to store wind, and never to be quite sure when it would emerge. Three – a strong body odour that no amount of deodorants could smother.

Chief Detective Marvin H. Slamish was not a happy man. He used mouthwash, underarm roll-ons, powders and sprays and female vaginal deodorants sprayed liberally over his private parts.

He still smelled lousy.

Fontaine got a whiff the moment he entered her apartment, 'Oh my God! What's that awful smell?' she said, turning up her nose in disgust.

Chief Detective Marvin H. Slamish winked, farted and removed his raincoat.

Fontaine was unamused. She gestured around her looted apartment, 'And exactly what are you going to do about this?' Her voice zinged with English authority. She glared at Chief Detective Slamish as though it was his own personal fault. 'Well?' her kaleidoscope eyes regarded him with disdain. 'Have you found my maid yet?'

Chief Detective Slamish slumped into a remaining chair, the stuffing bulging from where it had been ripped open. He had not had a good day. In fact his day had been pure shit. A drug bust that hadn't stuck. A row with his one-armed Vietnam war-veteran brother-in-law who was the biggest con artist in Manhattan. And now this stiff-assed English society broad. Wasn't it enough that his balls ached? Wasn't it enough that his strong odour was beginning to pervade even *his* insensitive nostrils?

'Everything's under control, ma'am,' he mumbled unconvincingly.

'Under control?' Fontaine arched incredulous eyebrows. 'Have you recovered my property? Have you arrested my maid?'

The two cops exchanged glances.

Slamish tried to summon an air of confidence and authority. 'Just give us time, ma'am, just give us time. An investigation is getting under way right now. In fact there are a few questions I'd like to ask you.'

'Questions? Me? You have to be kidding. I'm not the criminal in this case.'

'No you're not, ma'am. Then again it hasn't been unheard of for people to . . . er . . . arrange things. Insurance. You know what I mean?'

Fontaine's eyes blazed. 'Are you implying that I might have set this up myself?'

It was an unfortunate moment for Slamish to wink.

'You horrible little man!' Fontaine screamed. 'I'll have your badge for your . . . your impertinence!'

Wearily Slamish rose, farted, and attempted to apologize.

'Get out of here,' Fontaine stormed. 'I don't want you on my case. My husband is Benjamin Al Khaled and when I tell him of your accusations he'll have your badge!'

Chief Detective Slamish headed for the door. Some days it just wasn't worth getting out of bed.

* * *

Five long hours later Fontaine was comfortably installed in a suite at the Pierre Hotel. Thank God the bastards hadn't taken her jewellery. It had been safely locked up at the bank – a precaution Benjamin had always insisted on, and one that she had always followed.

As for the apartment, well it had needed decorating. And her clothes? A new wardrobe was never a problem, and fortunately she was adequately insured.

Yes. A couple of days at the Pierre while she got herself together and did some shopping.

Then home . . . London . . . Hobo . . . And a sorting-out of her life.

Chapter Three

Bernie Darrell had been divorced four months, two days and twelve hours exactly. He knew, because his ex-wife, Susanna, never tired of telephoning to let him know. Of course there were other reasons she telephoned. The pool was malfunctioning. Her Ferrari had broken down. Their child missed him. Was he really tasteless enough to be seen at Tips, a Beverly Hills club, with another woman? So soon? How did he think that made her feel?

He would never understand women. Susanna and he had spent a miserable five years as a married couple – in spite of how the gossip columns and fan magazines built them up as love's young dream.

Susanna Brent, beautiful young actress daughter of Carlos Brent, the famed singer/movie star/

31

rumoured Mafioso. And Bernie Darrell, the hot-shot record-company mogul.

Mogul! Him! That was a laugh! He had managed to keep Susanna in the style to which she was accustomed. Just. Only just. And she had never tired of throwing Daddy in his face, and how much better he was.

One morning Bernie had packed a suitcase, stacked it in the back of his silver Porsche, and fled. Susanna had been begging him to come back ever since.

Bernie didn't have much sense, but with the counsel of his friends, he'd realized that to go back was to present Susanna with his balls – on a plate – nicely garnished. The longer he stayed away, the more he knew this to be the truth.

He was lucky to have a friend like Nico Constantine. Nico had allowed him to move into his house with an invitation to stay as long as he wanted. So far he had stayed seven months, and enjoyed Nico's company so much that he had no desire to find a place of his own. Nico was his idol. He was everything that Bernie aspired to be. Bernie copied him religiously, only the result was not yet perfect.

At twenty-nine years of age Bernie had youth on his side. He was slim and athletic, and did all the good things such as playing tennis, jogging, working out at a gym. He also smoked grass profusely, sniffed coke constantly, and drank like a new generation

Dean Martin. Nico didn't touch drugs, and Bernie vowed he would give them up. But it was always tomorrow as far as he was concerned, and he never seemed to get around to tomorrow. Anyway he needed drugs, it was a social politeness. As boss of a West Coast record company, how could he sit around at a meeting with one of his groups and not indulge? Professional suicide.

Bernie attempted to imitate Nico's style of dress, but his suits were never the immaculate fit that Nico so effortlessly achieved, his shirts never lay correctly around the collar – even the hand-made ones. He looked fine – that is until he stood next to Nico.

Bernie had a handsome bland face, capped teeth, bad breath, permed hair, a scar on his stomach, a permanent suntan and a small penis.

One of the great things about Susanna was that in all their mud-slinging arguments she had never mentioned his little dick. Never. He loved her for that.

Now Bernie sat on a Las Vegas bound plane, staring out of the window, wondering how the hell he was going to explain Cherry to Nico.

Cherry sat beside him, elegant hands crossed primly on her lap. Beautiful face in repose. Long blonde hair hanging luxuriously down. Cherry was a knockout. Nico's knockout to be precise. Nico had dumped her a week ago with the usual roses and diamond trinket, and the usual speech about how he was only leaving her for her own good – and how much happier she would be without him.

What a bullshit artist Nico was. The absolute best. The original fuck-and-run merchant. He always left the girl thinking *she* had left *him*! Clever.

In seven months Bernie had seen him do it to six of them. All staggeringly beautiful in that newly scrubbed, wholesome young way. They all left without a whimper. Nico was right, they would be better off without him (quite why they never seemed to figure out) and they parted the best of friends, and wore his diamond trinket from Cartier (usually a mouse or a butterfly) and spoke about him in the most glowing of terms.

Bernie had never had that kind of luck with women. Whenever he tried to dump a girl they had hysterics, called him a motherfucking son-of-a-bitch bastard, and badmouthed him all over town.

What was he doing wrong?

'How long before we land?' Cherry asked sweetly.

Oh Christ! Cherry. She had turned up at the house looking for Nico. And she had been there when Nico had phoned from Vegas telling Bernie to grab some money and get on the next plane. Then, firmly, but of course with bags of innocent girlishness, she had insisted on coming too. 'I have to talk to Nico,' she explained. 'My life is at a crossroads, and only he can help me.'

'Can't you wait a coupla days?' Bernie had grumbled. 'He'll be back in L.A. before that.'

'No,' Cherry had insisted, 'I have to see him immediately.'

So he had been unable to shake Cherry. And what really bugged him was she'd allowed him to pay for her ticket. The nerve! Not one move towards her purse, just a sweet smile, a soft hand on his arm and a 'Thank you, Bernie.'

The thing was that everyone thought he was loaded. If he didn't know better he'd think so himself. The newspapers described him as Bernie Darrell, millionaire record boss. His company did OK. But millionaire? Forget it. He could barely scrape enough together to make Susanna's ludicrous alimony payments. And of course, being Carlos Brent's son-in-law, even though he was his *ex*-son-in-law, meant always having to pick up the check.

He wondered what Nico had meant by 'grab some money'. It seemed like a strange request coming from Nico. Nico was always flush, always the big spender. And in Vegas surely he could get as much credit as he could use? Anyway, Bernie had stopped by his office and extracted six-thousand dollars in cash from his safe. It occurred to him that ever since moving in with Nico he had never made any attempt to pay one household account. Even the liquor he ordered at the corner store he had them bill to the house. He felt guilty now, but Nico was truly the perfect host, and never expected a guest to put his hand in his pocket – even a seven-month guest.

Somewhere in the back of his mind Bernie knew that maybe something was amiss financially for Nico. A series of events pointed to this. Firstly, why had Nico suddenly sold his house two months previously? He got an excellent price, but everyone knew that if you had Beverly Hills real estate, the name of the game was to sit on it. Prices were escalating at an exciting rate.

Bernie had joked at the time, 'Trying to get rid of a permanent house guest, huh?'

Nico had smiled that enigmatic smile of his, and made all arrangements to move them over to the new house he had rented. No discomfort for anyone.

Then another thing Bernie had noticed, stacks of unpaid bills were starting to accumulate on Nico's desk, and Nico had always been meticulous at settling his accounts immediately.

Just little things, but enough to make Bernie wonder somewhere in the back of his mind – a place he didn't visit too often.

Cherry said, 'Oops! I'm not too fond of landings.'

She looked a little green. Bernie hoped she wasn't about to throw up, and sat back to enjoy the descent.

* * *

Nico had no sense of time. He had been sitting at the baccarat table how long? Two, three, four hours? He didn't know. He only knew that the losing streak he was on had no intention of quitting. A thin film of sweat skirted his brow, otherwise he was unaffected – his usual smiling, charming self.

His plan had gone disastrously wrong. What had started out as a fool-proof scheme to make a big killing – had turned into a joke. He'd lost every single dollar he'd made on his house. And even worse – he'd gone beyond that, and was now into the Casino for five-hundred-thousand-dollars.

So much for skill and talent and luck. If the cards and dice were against you there was nothing you could do. Except stop playing. And he hadn't done that. He'd kept right on going like some moron from the sticks.

He was now in a far more difficult situation than merely being broke. He was in debt to people who were hardly likely to be thrilled when they found out he couldn't pay up.

It was like a bad dream. It seemed to have happened before he knew it.

Two days. That's all it had taken.

The woman sitting beside him was pushing the

baccarat shoe towards him. She was winning quite heavily, and flirting with Nico, although she must have been well on her way toward being sixty. Her chubby arms and fingers were garnished with incredible jewellery – tasteless but effective. On her left hand she wore a gigantic diamond. Nico was fascinated by the size of it. It had to be worth at the very least five-hundred-thousand-dollars.

* * *

As the cab took them from the airport, Bernie was annoyed to note that Carlos Brent himself was head-lining at the Forum Hotel. Why the hell had Nico picked there?

'I've never been here before,' Cherry remarked, smoothing down her skirt with delicate pale hands.

'Don't get too comfortable,' Bernie muttered, 'you may be on the next plane back.'

'I don't think so,' replied Cherry. 'Nico will be happy to see me.'

Oh yeah? One thing Bernie knew about Nico was that once a broad was out she was out. No going back, however golden the muff.

Bernie was greeted regally at the reception desk. As Carlos Brent's ex-son-in-law he was a well-known figure at the Forum. He and Susanna had spent part of their honeymoon at the hotel. At the time Carlos was appearing there, and he had insisted that the whole wedding party flew back to Vegas with him to celebrate.

Shit! Making love to his new bride with her famous daddy in the adjoining penthouse had not been the greatest of experiences.

'I'd like to freshen up before I see Nico,' Cherry was saying.

'Sure,' Bernie agreed. 'Gimme the key to Nico Constantine's suite,' he instructed the girl behind the desk. 'It'll be fine, he's expecting us.'

'Certainly Mr Darrell,' she said, eyeing Cherry a from head to toe. News would have filtered over to Carlos that Bernie had arrived in Vegas with a nineteen-year-old blonde within the hour.

'This is Miss Cherry Lotte,' Bernie announced. 'Mr Constantine's fiancée.'

Fiancée! Sweet! What a lovely old-fashioned word.

Nico would kill him, but it was better than having Carlos Brent pissed off.

* * *

The baccarat shoe was emptied of cards by the bejewelled woman. Pass after pass she won, until the shoe was finished. She sorted out her stacks of chips with fat hands, and Nico was once again mesmerized by the size of her diamond ring.

He stood up. The pit boss said, 'Staying for another shoe, Mr Constantine?'

Nico forced a smile as he left the enclosure, 'I'll be back later.'

He felt sick to his stomach, then he saw Bernie hurrying toward him, and his spirits lifted. Bernie would have a way to bail him out. Bernie was a sharp kid, and anyway – after seven months of free everything, Bernie owed him a favour.

*　*　*

On the top floor of the Forum Hotel, Joseph Fonicetti kept his eye on the proceedings. He owned the Forum, and with the help of his two sons, Dino and David, he ran a tight ship. Not too much happened within the confines of the Forum that Joseph Fonicetti didn't know about.

For instance, the fourth girl on the right in the back chorus line had obtained an abortion the previous afternoon. She would be back at work tonight.

For instance, two waitresses in the Orgy Room were stealing – nickel-and-dime stuff. Joseph would keep them on, good waitresses were hard to find.

For instance, one of his pit bosses was planning to screw the casino manager's wife. That would have to be stopped immediately.

40

'What are we doing about Nico Constantine?' David asked his father.

'How much is he in to us for now?' Joseph replied, his eyes flicking across dozens of closed-circuit TV screens that showed him plenty of action.

David picked up a phone to get up-to-the-minute information.

'He's given us six-hundred-thousand of his money – and he's into us for five-hundred-and-ten-thousand. He just left the baccarat table and is meeting with Bernie Darrell.'

'I like Nico,' Joseph said softly, 'but no more than another fifty-thousand credit, and see that he pays us before he leaves Vegas. You take care of it, Dino.'

'Do we accept his cheque?' Dino asked.

Joseph closed his eyes, and thought for a minute. 'From Nico? Sure. Nico has plenty of money. Besides, he's too smart to ever try to shaft us. Nico Constantine without his balls – what kind of a ladies' man would that be?'

Chapter Four

Fontaine zipped through the New York stores at an alarming pace. When it came to shopping for clothes there was nobody better at spending money than her. She used her credit cards liberally, unworried that her lawyer in England had warned her to run up absolutely no more bills. She'd been robbed. Surely she was entitled to clothe herself for her imminent return to London? Armani, Valentino, Chanel – designer clothes had always suited her.

She had lunch with Allan Grant, Sarah's husband. He amused her, wanted to take her to bed for the afternoon. She demurred. She had more shopping to do. And she was to depart for London the very next day. She didn't want to hurt Allan's feelings, after all, she'd been to bed with him before, but he was simply not her style. At thirty-six he was too old. Why settle for an old model when you could have the very latest twenty-two-year-old actor with a body like Ryan Gosling?

Fontaine had always been able to attract any man she wanted. Men could not resist the lure of her perfumed thighs. Besides which, she possessed that rare commodity – good old-fashioned glamour – and men, especially young men, loved it.

She left Allan, and went shopping at Bendels, where she purchased two pairs of boots at eight-hundred dollars apiece. A simple black crocodile shoulder bag – twelve-thousand dollars. An art deco necklace and earrings – two-thousand dollars. And six-hundred dollars' worth of make-up and perfume.

She charged everything, and ordered it sent special delivery to her hotel. Then she decided that she really must get some rest before the evening's activities, so she took a taxi to the Pierre, where she had a long luxurious bubble bath, carefully applied a special cucumber face mask, and slept for three and a half hours.

* * *

Jump Jennings checked out his appearance one more time before leaving his seedy apartment in the

Village. He looked good, he knew that. Only the question was – did he look good enough? Tonight was the night to find out.

Jump had been christened Arthur George Jennings, but he had been nicknamed Jump in high school because of his athletic prowess, and it had sort of stuck. Jump wasn't a bad name to be stuck with either. Jump Jennings. It sounded pretty good. It would look pretty good one day – high up on a marquee in lights next to Clooney or Pitt. The world would be ready for Jump. His time would come. He hoped desperately that his time would come that very night.

He hitched up his black leather trousers, and adjusted the collar of his black leather bomber jacket. He was going for a Sylvester Stallone look. Yeah – and it suited him too.

Confident at last, he left his apartment.

* * *

Fontaine awoke an hour before her date was due to pick her up. She relished the thought of an exciting evening ahead. An art gallery opening, two parties, then the inevitable hot club, where anything could happen and usually did.

She dressed with care after applying impeccable make-up. She wore a deep V-necked brown satin wrap dress, tightly belted over narrow crêpe de chine trousers. Strappy high-heeled pewter-coloured sandals completed the look.

One of Leslie's juniors arrived to comb out her hair, and by the time he was finished teasing and crimping, she looked a knockout.

Of course the diamonds and emeralds she was wearing helped. They always did.

Jump Jennings turned up on time. Fontaine shuddered at his choice of outfit. He looked like a refugee from the Hells Angels. Would her friends laugh? After all there was such a thing as going too far.

'Don't you have a suit?' she asked rather testily.

'Wassamatter with the leather?' Jump questioned aggressively.

'It's very . . . macho. But a suit might be more . . . well right. Something Italian, double breasted perhaps.'

Jump narrowed his eyes. 'Lady, you wanted me in a suit, you should've bought me one. I'm an actor, not a fuckin' fashion plate.'

And so their evening began. Jump, broody and discontented. Fontaine, ever so slightly embarrassed by her escort.

Several glasses of champagne later she couldn't have cared less. So what if he wore leather? He was six feet tall and had muscles in places other men didn't even have places. He would do very nicely to round off the evening with.

Jump was doing his best early Depp, and it was knocking everyone sideways. Boy, he could've laid every woman in the place – they all looked like they could do with a satisfying bang. Instead he concentrated all of his energies on Fontaine. She was some foxy lady.

They'd met the previous week at a party in the Village, and she'd whisked him back to her apartment in a chauffeur-driven limo real quick. Once there, they had indulged in a four-hour sex marathon that had taxed even Jump's giant strength. Wow! Some wild woman! And rich. And classy. And stylish. He was sick of dumb twenty-year-olds anyway. He wanted her to take him to London with her. He ached to go to Europe.

'Having fun?' Fontaine murmured, sneaking up behind him.

'Beats jackin' off,' he retorted.

She smiled. 'Oh my, you're so crude.'

'An' you like it.'

'Sometimes.'

'Always,' he said, his hand sliding across her backside.

She pushed him away. 'Not here,' she admonished.

'You'd like it anywhere,' he said with a knowing leer.

'I knew there was something about you that I found irresistible,' she said coolly. 'I guess it's your perception and intelligence.'

He moved close to her and licked his lips. 'Naw – it's my cock!' he said crudely.

Fontaine merely smiled.

* * *

They made love for hours. It seemed like hours. It probably *was* hours.

Fontaine lay in bed, her head propped against the pillows, a cigarette in one hand. She was covered by a sheet in the semi-dark hotel room. Outside she could hear the occasional whining of police sirens and the usual New York street noises.

Jump was curled in the foetal position at the foot of the bed. He was asleep, his muscled body twitching with occasional nervous spasms. He snored lightly.

Fontaine wished he'd gone home. She didn't enjoy them staying the night. Why couldn't they just get dressed and go? In all honesty the only man she had ever enjoyed spending the night with was her ex-husband, Benjamin, and that was strictly a non-sexual thing. Oh yes – they had made love on occasion, but Benjamin's stamina was low. To put it crudely, a two-minute erection was about all he could manage. So she had looked elsewhere for sex. And who could blame her? However, Benjamin had been a friendly all-night companion, in spite of the fact that business calls came through from all over the world every night which hadn't been too much fun. But still, she missed the basic companionship for at one time Benjamin *had* cared about her.

What did this muscled lump lying at the bottom of her bed care about? Certainly not her, that was for sure. Oh maybe he liked her, was in awe of her, thought she could help him in some way. But care? Forget it. Most of the sexual athletes of this world were users. They bargained with their bodies, and she should know – she'd done it herself many times.

With a sigh Fontaine got up and made her way into the bathroom. She gazed at her reflection in the mirror. Her hair was a mess, and her make-up smudged. Good. Maybe Jump – what a ridiculous name – would take one look at her and leave. *I must be getting old*, she thought, with a wry smile, *if all I have in mind is getting rid of him.*

She ran the shower, and lingered beneath the icy needles of water.

Jump stirred and awoke. He reached for Fontaine's leg, groped around, and realized that she wasn't there. He was annoyed with himself for falling asleep. After the sex should have come the talk. He was all ready to hurry back to his apartment, throw some clothes in a bag, and jet off to London with Fontaine. What would an extra ticket matter to her? Anyway, he would give her plenty of value for money.

He could hear the sound of the shower. Leaping off the bed he padded into the bathroom.

Fontaine's body was silhouetted through the shower curtain. Jump didn't hesitate, he climbed right in with her. His entrance was spoiled by the fact that he hadn't realized it was a cold shower, and it took exactly two seconds for his powerful erection to become a shrivelled inch and a half!

Fontaine couldn't help laughing. Jump was mortified.

By the time he recovered, Fontaine was briskly towelling herself dry. She brushed him away with a curt, 'Not now, I have to pack.'

Jump seized his last chance. 'How's about taking me with you?' he suggested. 'We could have ourselves a real good time.'

Fontaine had a fleeting vision of returning to London with a twenty-year-old leather-clad dumb actor. Not exactly the image she wished to project.

'Jump,' she said kindly, 'one of the first things an actor should learn how to do is to make a graceful exit. You played your part beautifully, but, darling, this is the end of the New York run, and London is not exactly beckoning.'

Jump scowled. He didn't know what the hell she was talking about, however, he recognized a no when he heard one.

Chapter Five

'Cherry?' Nico's glared at Bernie, 'Why the hell did you bring her?'

They sat in the bar lounge together, Bernie had never seen Nico so angry.

'I had no choice,' he explained weakly. 'She was there when you called, and she just kinda insisted.'

'There is always a choice in life,' Nico said coldly, gazing off into space as he sipped his vodka.

Bernie coughed nervously. 'So,' he ventured, 'what's happening? We having fun?'

'We're having shit,' Nico retorted. 'How much money did you bring?'

Bernie patted his jacket pocket. 'Six-thousand dollars. We going to play it?'

Nico laughed mirthlessly. 'I have already played it

my friend. I am indebted to this very fine casino to the tune of five-hundred-and-fifty-thousand dollars. And that is not to mention the six-hundred-thousand of my own that I lost upfront.'

Bernie sniggered as if he didn't quite believe what he was hearing. 'What is this? Some kind of a joke?' he asked.

'No joke,' Nico snapped. 'The truth. Feel free to call me any kind of dumbass you like.'

They sat in uneasy silence for a few minutes, then Bernie said, 'Listen, Nico, since when did you become the last of the great gamblers? I mean I've seen you play enough times and you've never been into heavy stakes.'

Nico nodded. 'What can I tell you? I got greedy, and I guess when you get greedy your luck flies out of the window. Right, my friend?'

Bernie nodded. He'd seen it happen before. When gambling fever hit, sometimes there was nothing you could do about it. It carried you along with a force that was breathtaking. Win or lose you couldn't stop.

'How are you going to pay them?' he asked.

'I can't,' Nico replied calmly.

'Jesus! Don't even kid around on the subject.'

'Who's kidding? I can't pay, it's as simple as that.'

'The Fonicettis would never have given you that

kind of credit if they didn't know you were good for it.'

Nico nodded. 'I realize that now. But at the time I wasn't thinking straight, and nobody put a limit on my markers. I suppose they figured if I could lose six-hundred-grand of my own, then I didn't exactly have a cash-flow problem. The six-hundred was my house. My final stake. I'm broke, kid, busted out.'

The full enormity of Nico's dilemma was only just occurring to Bernie. To lose was bad enough. But not to be able to pay . . . well, that was suicide, pure undiluted suicide. Everybody knew what happened to bad debtors. Bernie personally knew a guy in L.A. who had owed the bookies seven-thousand dollars. Seven-thousand measly dollars, for crissakes. He'd been washed up on Malibu beach one morning, and the word had gone around that he was 'an example'. A lot of outstanding debts had been settled that week.

'You're in trouble,' Bernie said.

'An understatement,' Nico agreed.

'We'll figure something out,' Bernie replied, and as he spoke, his mind was already checking out the limited possibilities.

* * *

Cherry ran around Nico's suite full of childish delight. She even jumped up and down on the huge bed, and blushed when she thought of the fun they could have on it later.

Cherry had been in Los Angeles a little over a year, but already she'd decided that the hustle and grind of being an actress was not for her. She had been a successful model in Texas when the call of Hollywood had brought her to a modest apartment on Fountain Avenue. Twenty-five auditions, two bit parts, and a commercial later, she'd met Nico. Love had entered Cherry's life for the first time.

Sex had already entered it. First in high school with the football pro. Secondly with a blue jeans manufacturer. Thirdly with a Hollywood agent who promised her big things. She saw big things, but they weren't exactly what she'd had in mind.

Nico was something else. He was everything she had always imagined a man should be. He was Rhett Butler, from *Gone With the Wind*, and Jay Gatsby from *The Great Gatsby*. He was special and exciting and very sexy. Cherry always looked at life through the movies, things seemed more real that way.

Nico had swept her off her feet, from the moment they met at a party, to the moment he gave her his famous farewell speech.

At first she had cried then realized how right he

was. Then she'd thought, *Why is he right? Why will I be happier without him?*

Then the thought had occurred to her that without him she was miserable, so it stood to reason they should be together. Immediately she'd rushed over to his house to tell him this exciting news, but he wasn't there, and Bernie had been kind enough to invite her to Las Vegas to find him.

She washed her hands, brushed her long golden hair, and sat and waited patiently. But after two hours she wondered if maybe she should go and look for them.

After checking her perfect appearance one final time, she set off to the elevator.

* * *

Dino Fonicetti had often been told he was the absolute image of a young Al Pacino. It was true. He was the best-looking goddamn guinea in the whole of goddamn Las Vegas, and as such he had his pick of the girls. Not that appearance had that much to do with sexual success. His brother David had the misfortune to look like a Mack truck, and David also scored with monotonous regularity.

Dino entered the elevator, and was stopped in his tracks by just about the most exquisite-looking female he had ever seen.

It was the delectable and innocent-looking Cherry.

Dino couldn't stop staring. 'Hello there,' he said.

Cherry gazed demurely at the floor.

Dino, master of the fast one liner racked his brains for something to say. He came up with, 'Are you staying at the hotel?'

Not a bad opening. Not particularly good either.

Cherry looked at him with wide blue eyes. 'I'm just visiting,' she said primly.

Some answer. Everyone was just visiting in Las Vegas.

The elevator reached lobby level and stopped. They both stepped out. Cherry hesitated.

'Where you headed?' Dino asked.

'I'm meeting a friend,' Cherry replied, wondering who this handsome man was.

Dino decided he couldn't allow this exquisite girl to walk out of his life. He extended his hand. 'I'm Dino Fonicetti. My family owns this hotel and if there is anything at all I can do for you, anything at all, don't hesitate to ask.'

Her hand, as she gripped his, felt soft and small. He was in love. Pow! Just like that, he was getting a hard-on.

'I'm trying to locate Mr Nico Constantine. Do you know him?' Her voice was soft and low, almost as delectable as her hand.

Did he know Nico? Why, Nico was the very man he was looking for himself.

Did *she* know Nico? *Shit!*

*   *   *

Nico and Bernie were still in a huddle discussing the possibilities, when Bernie said, 'I don't believe what I'm seeing. Dino Fonicetti is heading our way hand in hand with Cherry.'

Nico glanced up, then stood as they approached the table.

Dino was indeed leading Cherry by the hand, determined not to let go of her. She went with him meekly, heads turning as she passed.

She gazed at Nico, her eyes brimming over with the emotion of the moment. 'I had to come,' she murmured softly. 'I missed you so.'

Nico's eyes flicked quickly between her and Dino.

'I met Mr Fonicetti in the elevator,' Cherry continued. 'He was kind enough to help me look for you.'

'Nico!' Dino exclaimed warmly.

'Dino!' Nico's greeting was equally warm.

'And Bernie,' Dino added, 'why didn't you let me know you were coming?'

Bernie shrugged. 'Didn't know I was until today.'

'Are you comfortable? Is everything all right?' Dino asked.

Nico nodded. 'Perfect,' he said.

'Let me know if there's anything you need,' Dino said. 'And by the way, how long will you be staying?'

The question was casual enough, but Nico knew why it was asked. 'Long enough to recover some of my money,' he joked.

'Sure, sure.' Dino flashed his best Pacino smile. 'We like everyone to leave here winners. Now tonight I want you all to be my guests for dinner.' He looked at Cherry. 'We'll catch Carlos Brent's late supper show. You'd like that, wouldn't you?'

Cherry glanced at Nico. He nodded.

As a parting shot Dino turned to Bernie. 'Susanna's here,' he said. 'She looks great.' Then he strolled off.

'Who gives a shit,' Bernie muttered angrily.

Cherry asked, 'Who's Susanna?'

'Nobody important,' Bernie growled. 'Just my ex-wife.'

Nico was busily counting out money. He handed Cherry a few hundred dollars. 'Be a good girl, run along and play something. Bernie and I have things to discuss.'

'Nico,' she said, almost pleading, 'I really want to talk to you. I have some very important things to say. I came all this way just to—'

'I didn't ask you to come,' he said irritably.

Her eyes filled with tears. 'I thought you'd be pleased.'

'Sure I'm pleased, hon, but right now I'm busy.'

Cherry pouted. 'I don't know how to gamble.'

Nico pointed out Dino talking to one of the pit bosses. 'Your friend will teach you. I got a feeling he'll be only too delighted to show you how it's done.' Cherry departed reluctantly, and Bernie and Nico exchanged glances. 'I think little Cherry is going to work in our favour,' Nico said.

'Right,' Bernie agreed. 'I haven't seen Dino this excited since he got laid by the entire Forum chorus line on two consecutive nights!'

Nico laughed. 'Let's go over the plan one more time.'

* * *

Dino offered Cherry more wine. She declined, holding a delicate hand over her glass to prevent him from filling it. 'I never drink more than one glass,' she said solemnly.

'Never?' Dino chided.

'Never,' Cherry replied. 'Unless it's a wedding or a big event.'

'This *is* a big event,' Dino insisted, moving her hand and filling her glass to the brim. He felt elated at the way things were turning out. Nico had practically handed over Cherry on a plate. The four of

61

them had eaten together, then Nico had taken Dino to one side and explained that he had a late date, and that Cherry arriving in Vegas had been an embarrassment that he didn't need. Dino had assured him not to worry, he would be more than happy to take care of Cherry.

'She's a wonderful girl,' Nico had enthused. 'Only she's no more than a sister to me now, and yet I wouldn't want to hurt her feelings. I'll probably spend the night with my date.'

'I'll make sure Cherry never finds out,' Dino said, thinking that if he could persuade Cherry to spend the night with him, how *could* she find out? And who cared anyway, Cherry was now his.

After dinner Nico had made an excuse and left, and then Bernie had been set upon by his ex-wife, Susanna, and gone off in a huddle with her, now it was just Cherry and Dino.

Cherry was confused, but determined to help Nico out. He'd asked her to keep Dino busy. 'Do anything, but be sure he is totally absorbed by you until at least noon tomorrow.' Nico had said, kissing her softly. 'It's important to me; one day I'll explain it to you.'

Cherry sipped her wine slowly. 'Dino?' she questioned. 'Do you actually live in the hotel, or do you have a house?'

'I live right here, babe,' Dino said proudly. 'There

are five penthouses, and one of them is all mine. Best view of the Strip you're ever likely to see – that's if you'd like to see it.'

'Ooh, I'd simply love to. Can I?'

Could she? Goddamn. Things were working out better than he'd hoped.

Dino's full concentration was on Cherry. He forgot about everything else. Going to bed with this exquisite little doll was his prime concern. He quite forgot that he was supposed to quiz Nico about his markers and get his personal cheque to cover them. Five-hundred-thousand big ones was quite a debt by anyone's standards. But still, getting to know Cherry was enough to take anyone's mind off anything. And it wasn't like Nico was taking off anywhere, he was around. Dino decided he would talk to him about it the following day.

* * *

As soon as he made his excuses at the dinner and was able to get away, Nico headed straight for the casino. He scanned the room searching for the lady who was to be his date.

Mrs Dean Costello scooped in another stack of five-hundred-dollar chips; she was having fun. She considered it a shame Mr Dean Costello hadn't dropped off a few years earlier, he'd been so stingy with his massive fortune. Hadn't he realized that money was there to have fun with?

Whoops – up came another number. Thirty-five. She had five chips on the centre and a cheval all round it.

'You're very lucky tonight,' Nico said, coming up behind her.

She turned to see who was speaking, and there stood the handsome man from the baccarat table.

'I suppose I am,' she said, raking in her chips.

Nico watched her giant diamond ring catch the lights and sparkle invitingly. It had to be worth enough to get him out of trouble. He wondered how much she weighed. Two-hundred or three-hundred pounds? Somewhere between the two. He wondered how old she was. Fifty? Maybe even sixty.

'You're a beautiful woman,' he muttered in her ear, 'and beautiful women shouldn't waste a night like tonight at the gaming tables.'

'Are you foreign?' she asked, flattered by his compliments but not surprised. Mrs Dean Costello thought that she was indeed beautiful. A few pounds overweight perhaps, and a little old for some tastes. But this guy was no chicken, and he knew a good-looking mature sexual woman when he saw one. He was no fool.

She began to cash in her chips. Opportunities like this did not happen every day.

A half hour later they were in her suite. When Nico wanted something he did not waste time.

'I don't usually invite strange men up to my room.' Mrs Costello giggled.

'I'm not strange,' Nico replied, opening up a bottle of champagne and surreptitiously slipping two strong sleeping pills into her glass. 'What is so strange about wanting to be alone with a beautiful woman?'

Mrs Costello cackled with delight. This was some hot guy – the best one to come her way since the twenty-year-old waiter in Detroit.

* * *

Susanna had not been part of the plan – but what could Bernie do? She grabbed his arm, bossy as ever, and lectured him in an increasingly whiney voice about what a sonofabitch his lawyer was. Bernie sat and nodded, hardly able to get a word in. He watched Dino and Cherry at a nearby table, it all seemed to be going well.

Susanna tugged his arm. 'I said what are you doing here? Aren't you listening to me?'

'Sure,' he said, snapping back to attention and focusing on Susanna. She had her mother's sharp features softened by an excellent nose job.

'Well?' She glared at him.

'I didn't think I needed your permission to come to Vegas.'

'That's right, give me one of your smartass answers, that's all you're capable of,' Susanna sneered.

Bernie stood up. He didn't need this crap. 'You'll have to excuse me, Susanna. I have a hot date with a black-jack dealer. The cards are calling, that's why I came here.'

'Gambling!' Susanna spat. 'While I have to fight you for every stinking cent of my alimony.'

He threw her a cold look. He was paying her plenty, and she was insisting on more. It was a joke. Carlos Brent was worth millions and Susanna was his only child. Out of the corner of his eye he saw Cherry and Dino rise from their table.

'Gotta go,' he said quickly.

'Bernie,' Susanna restrained him with a hand on his arm, her voice softening, 'why don't we get together for a drink later? I'm really sick of all the arguments.'

Christ! More complications! Susanna had that 'I wanna get laid' aura about her.

Bernie managed an encouraging look. 'I'd like that. Where will you be?'

'I'm spending some time with Daddy after the show, then I'll be in my room. Come for a drink.'

'Right. I'll see you later.' He made his escape just in time to watch Cherry and Dino getting into the elevator. The kid had really come up trumps – one word from Nico and she was prepared to do anything to help.

Bernie hurried outside. He had his part to do as well.

They all wanted to help Nico.

Chapter Six

New York's Kennedy airport was as busy as ever. The weather hadn't been pleasant, and a lot of people were sitting around and complaining, waiting for their flights to take off.

Fontaine Khaled arrived at the airport in her usual style. She swept in, followed by two porters organizing her luggage.

An airport official rushed over immediately.

Jump hovered in the background thinking about the day he would get treated in such a fashion.

'Mrs Khaled. Delighted to see you again,' said the official.

'Check me in?' Fontaine said, in no mood for small talk.

'Of course, of course. Would you care to wait in our VIP lounge?'

Fontaine was irritated. 'There's not a delay is there?'

'Only slight.'

'Christ!'

The airport official signalled to an airline representative. 'Escort Mrs Khaled to the lounge.'

'Lets go,' Fontaine beckoned Jump with an imperious wave of her hand.

* * *

Nico's flight from Los Angeles had arrived one hour previously. He was not delighted to discover that his on-going flight to London was delayed. He sat in the VIP lounge sipping vodka and musing on the events that had led him to where he was. He felt strangely elated when he really should be scared shitless. Maybe he had been stagnating for the last ten years. What had seemed like a good time had certainly not sent the adrenaline coursing through his veins like it was now.

Bernie had been helpful. It had been Bernie's suggestion that if Nico couldn't pay his markers he should take off.

'Don't stay around to explain,' Bernie had urged him. 'Skip the hell out. Get the money – and don't let them find you till you have it.'

Wise advice. However Nico had no idea how he was going to get the money. Then it came to him, an idea so out of character and yet so obvious. He would steal the fat woman's ring – it had to be worth at least as much as he'd lost.

At first Bernie had thought he was kidding. Then he saw that Nico was indeed serious, and his mind had started to work. Steal the ring. Get the hell out of Vegas without the Fonicettis knowing. Sell the ring. Pay off the markers – and then worry about compensating the fat woman, for Nico insisted that she must be paid back.

It was a risky plan, but they both decided it would work.

Dino's crush on Cherry took care of him watching Nico too closely, and Cherry had entered into the spirit of the caper with great enthusiasm. Bernie hired a car. Once Nico had the ring, he took the car, drove back to Los Angeles, picked up some clothes and headed straight for the airport.

Bernie had a friend in London, Hal, who had connections, and would be able to get the right deal on the ring. London was far enough away for Nico to have time to do what he had to do. By the time the Fonicettis realized he had left Vegas, he would be back with the money.

Of course the plan had holes. The fat woman would probably start hollering the moment she awoke from her drug-induced sleep. But Nico had given her a false name, and who would suspect him anyway? He had made sure that they left the casino separately, and their only connection was sitting next to each other at the baccarat table.

Bernie and Cherry would stay in Vegas, and make believe Nico was still there too.

Now Nico waited for his connecting flight, and fingered the ring lying loosely in his pocket. He was concerned about customs. What if they stopped him and found it? Not a good thought.

A woman swept into the lounge. She was sophisticated, assured and beautiful. Early forties, very expensive, totally in control. Almost a female version of himself. He couldn't help smiling at the thought. She was accompanied by a muscle-bound young man who hung on to her every word. And her every word was very audible, as she spoke in a piercing voice that didn't give a damn about who might be listening.

'God! This is all so boring!' she said loudly. 'Why can't the bloody plane take off when it's supposed to?' She threw herself dramatically into a chair, shrugged off her sable coat, and crossed silken legs. 'Do order some champagne, darling.'

'Who is that?' Nico asked the waiter serving drinks.

The waiter shrugged. 'Fontaine Khaled. Some Arab billionaire's wife. We have instructions to look after her. She's been through here before and she's an absolute bitch.'

* * *

Sitting in the airport lounge Fontaine decided that it was time for Jump to leave. He was annoying her. He was so obvious it was pathetic. All those little hints about how he longed to go to Europe. How he would miss her desperately. How she was bound to miss him. And hadn't their love-making been the most erotic and sensual experience ever.

'You shouldn't hang around here any longer,' Fontaine said abruptly. 'I might try to catch a nap.'

'I can't leave you,' Jump replied. 'The flight could be delayed or cancelled. I don't mind staying.'

Of course he didn't mind staying. He was hoping she would change her mind and take him with her.

'No, I insist.' Fontaine said firmly. 'You've been here quite long enough.'

Jump stood his ground. 'I'll stay, Fontaine. You never know what might happen.'

Before she could reply a hostess appeared and announced that the flight was ready to board.

'About time,' Fontaine complained, standing up and allowing Jump to adjust her sable coat around her shoulders.

He moved in, going for a passionate embrace. She dodged the embrace and offered him her cheek to kiss. 'Not in public,' she murmured. 'I do have a certain reputation.'

'When will you call me?' he asked anxiously, more concerned about a trip to London than her reputation.

'Soon enough,' she replied succinctly, muttering to herself, 'But don't hold your breath.'

* * *

Nico secured the seat next to Mrs Khaled for two reasons. One, who better than to unwittingly carry his diamond through British customs than an English woman who it seemed unlikely they would stop. Two, the flight ahead was long and boring, and while Mrs Khaled was slightly older than his admittedly juvenile tastes, she at least looked like she could amuse him, and if his luck was in perhaps play a passable game of backgammon.

He allowed Fontaine to settle into her window seat before taking his place.

She glanced over at him, amazing kaleidoscope eyes summing him up.

He smiled, full Nico charm. 'Allow me to introduce myself, Nico Constantine.'

She raised a cynical eyebrow, he was attractive, but

much too old for her, and she wasn't in the mood for a conversation.

Nico was not to be brushed off. 'And you are . . . ?'

'Mrs Khaled,' she replied shortly. 'And I may as well warn you, that even though we are travelling companions for the next few hours, I am totally exhausted, and certainly not in the mood for polite conversation. You do understand, Mr . . . er . . .'

'Constantine. And of course I understand. But perhaps I can offer you some champagne?'

'You can offer away. Only let us not forget that they serve it free in first class.'

'I meant when we arrive in London. Perhaps dinner at Annabel's?'

Fontaine frowned. How crass to have to cope with a man on the make when all she wanted to do was sleep. She glanced across the aisle at a thirtyish blonde in a striped mink coat. 'Try her,' she said coldly. 'I think you'll have more success.'

Nico followed her glance. 'Dyed hair, too much make-up, no style. Please credit me with some taste.'

Oh, God! What had she done to be stuck next to this man? She turned and stared out of the window. Perhaps she should have brought Jump, if only to protect her from bores on planes.

'Your seat belt,' he said.

'Excuse me?'

'The sign is on.'

She fiddled for her seat belt, couldn't find one half of it Nico realized, and attempted to help her buckle up.

'I can manage, thank you,' she snapped.

Nico was perplexed. A woman who did not respond to his charm? Impossible. Unheard of. For ten years he had taken his pick of the best that Hollywood had to offer. Ripe juicy young beauties – at his beck and call day and night. Never a turn down. Always adoration. And now this . . . this English woman. So full of herself, waspish, and frankly a pain in the ass.

Still, if he wanted to plant the diamond on her, then he had to develop a line of communication.

The plane was taxiing down the runway preparing for take-off.

'Are you a nervous flyer?' Nico asked.

Fontaine shot him a scornful look. 'Hardly. I have been flying since I was sixteen years old. God knows how many flights I have taken.' She shut her eyes. How many flights *had* she taken? Plenty. The first year of her marriage to Benjamin she had accompanied him everywhere. The perfect wife. Trips all over the world, boring business trips that had driven her mad, until at last she had begged off and only taken the interesting ones. Paris. Rome. Rio. New York. Acapulco. Marvellous shopping. Exciting friends.

And then the lovers. Well, Benjamin had driven her to the lovers.

She felt the thrust as the big plane became airborne, but she kept her eyes tightly shut, didn't want to encourage her travelling companion to indulge in any more inane conversation. He was an attractive man. Not her type of course, much too ancient. Probably appeal to her friend Vanessa, who liked them a little worn.

* * *

'You've been asleep for two hours,' Nico announced.

Fontaine opened her eyes slowly. She felt hot and creased, and the taste in her mouth was truly vile.

Nico handed her a glass of champagne. She sipped it gratefully.

'Do you play backgammon?' he asked.

'So that's what you are,' she said, and she couldn't help smiling. 'A backgammon hustler! I should have known.'

Nico grinned. 'A backgammon player, yes. A backgammon hustler, no. Sorry to disappoint you.'

'You look the part, my God, you're almost better dressed than I am!'

'That would be impossible.'

Suddenly they were talking and laughing. The stewardess served food and more champagne.

He wasn't so bad, Fontaine decided. Rather nice actually. And what a refreshing change to have a conversation with a man who was neither gay nor a young stud. Idly she wondered if he had money. He was certainly dressed well enough – and his watch was expensive and in perfect taste.

'What business are you in?' she asked casually.

Nico smiled. 'Commodities.'

'That sounds like it could be anything.'

'It usually is, I don't like to be pinned down.'

'Hmm . . .' She fixed him with a quizzical look. 'And you? Where is Mr Khaled?'

'Benjamin Al Khaled no longer has the pleasure of calling himself my husband. Ex is the word, keep it to yourself, I get better service when the world doesn't know.'

Nico looked her over admiringly. 'I'm sure a beautiful woman like you would always get good service.'

'Thank you.'

Their eyes met and locked. There was that moment when nothing is said but everything is known.

Fontaine broke the look. Maybe it was the plane trip, maybe she was overtired, but suddenly she felt incredibly horny.

'Excuse me,' she got up and moved past him to visit the toilet. She wanted to check out her appearance. She probably looked a mess, and that wouldn't do at all.

Nico watched her go, and sniffed at the cloud of Opium perfume she left behind. Lise Maria had always worn Jolie Madame. It was the first time he had thought of his late wife in a long time. Lise Maria belonged in the past, wrapped in a beautiful memory he did not care to disturb. Why was he thinking of her now?

'Will you be watching the movie, Mr Constantine?' the flight attendant enquired.

'What is it?'

'The latest George Clooney.'

'Sure – leave the earphones.'

'And Mrs Khaled?'

'Yes. Mrs Khaled will watch it too.'

Making decisions for her already! And thinking about how it would be in bed with a woman like that. It had been so long since he'd had a real woman. Plenty of girls – gorgeous sweet creatures who enjoyed his expert tuition. But to have a real woman again, a sophisticated sensual female . . .

Idly he wondered if she had money, what a plus *that* would be.

Chapter Seven

Polly Brand stirred in her sleep and reached out. Her arm encountered flesh, and she awoke with a start. Then she remembered, grinned, and reached for her glasses. 'All the better to see you with, my dear!' She giggled, as she trailed her fingers down her companion's back.

'Get off,' he mumbled, still half asleep.

'Oh come on,' Polly responded, full of enthusiasm. 'We've just got time to do it before we go to the airport.'

'Do what?'

'It, of course.' Her hand reached for his slumbering penis.

He moved away. 'I gotta sleep. Ten more minutes.'

'Ricky, I've landed you a plum job, and I do expect you to be grateful, very grateful in fact.'

'I'll be fucking grateful tonight,' he mumbled. 'Right now I need to sleep.'

Polly squirmed all over him. 'You'll be working tonight, Ricky Tick. Our Mrs Khaled will have you hard at it ferrying her around till all hours. The bitch never sleeps. She has to be seen constantly, and your chauffeur duties will not be over till dawn. And that's when I like to sleep. So come on, let's fuck!'

Reluctantly Ricky allowed the energetic Polly to go to work on him until he was in a ready state to do her bidding.

A six-minute thrash around the bed and it was over.

'Thanks a lot,' complained Polly. 'Is that all you got?'

'Morning's not my best time,' Ricky muttered, reaching for his watch. 'Especially not five a bleedin' clock.'

'We have to be at the airport by seven. Mrs Khaled cannot be kept waiting, she'll throw a right fit if she is. Your new employer is very temperamental.'

'Can't wait. Are you sure this job isn't just one big drag?'

Polly giggled. 'You'll love it. You'll have a great time. If I know dear old Fontaine . . .'

'Yeah?'

Polly climbed out of bed still giggling. 'Just wait and see, you're in for a big surprise. If she likes you that is. And oh boy, I've got a hunch she'll like you a lot.'

Fontaine Khaled and Ricky the chauffeur. The thought sent Polly off into gales of laughter.

Ricky followed her out of bed. 'Come on, share the joke, luv.'

'You'll know soon enough.' Polly clicked on her iPod and the sound of Rod Stewart filled the room. She proceeded to exercise to his voice, unconcernedly naked.

Ricky watched her for a minute, then he hurried into the bathroom. Funny little thing that one. She had chatted him up in his mini-cab two weeks earlier, and before he knew it he had quit his job to accept the position as Mrs Khaled's chauffeur. Well, driving a mini-cab was not for him. Too many bleedin' headaches. Now chauffeuring was another thing, if a bloke had to drive around London day and night he may as well do it in a Roller.

Polly stretched her arms to the ceiling, then back to touch the floor. 'Twenty-four, twenty-five, finished,' she announced.

She couldn't be bothered to wash, a bad habit but no one had ever complained. She pulled on a fluffy angora sweater and tight jeans, knee-length boots, and dragged a comb through her short spiky hair. Make-up was lip gloss only. Her tinted glasses did the rest. Polly was not pretty – more unusual and certainly attractive. She was twenty-nine years old, and head of her own public relations firm. Not bad for a girl who started out as a secretary at seventeen. Her firm represented Fontaine Khaled's nightclub, Hobo, and Mrs Khaled called on her whenever she needed anything. Polly didn't mind. For each service she performed she added a little extra on the bill. Finding Ricky would be worth at least a couple of hundred.

He emerged from the bathroom clad in a pair of jockey shorts decorated with a garish picture of a rhinoceros and a slogan saying 'I feel horny'.

'Christmas! Where did you get those?' Polly said as she fell about laughing.

'My kid sister.' Ricky walked over to the mirror to admire himself. 'They look all right, don't they?'

'All right? They're a fucking scream!'

Ricky frowned. 'It's only a joke, no need to wet your panties.'

Polly tried to stop laughing. 'I didn't know guys actually wore things like that.'

Ricky's dignity was affronted. He pulled on his pants and glared at her.

Polly leaned back and studied him through narrowed eyes. Great body. Thin, wiry, rock-hard thighs and stomach, and a nice tight ass. Sexy, sexy face, dirty-blond hair and, when he was in the mood, a natural enthusiasm for screwing. Nice and normal.

Not into grass or coke or tying you to the bed. Probably didn't even know what bondage was.

Fontaine Khaled, if she felt like it, would absolutely adore him.

* * *

The interior of the plane was dark as the big jet winged its way towards England. The movie had finished, and now most of the passengers were asleep.

Fontaine wasn't.

Nico wasn't.

They were indulging in a necking session, teenage in its intensity.

Who could ever forget the excitement of one's first furtive gropings? The hands under the sweater, up the skirt. The lips, tongues, teeth. The eroticism of investigating a strange ear. The exquisite thrill of a clandestinely fondled nipple.

Fontaine felt as flushed as any fifteen-year-old. It was an amazing sensation.

Nico, too, was filled with an unremembered excitement. To touch but not to be really able to. To feel, but not properly.

Whoever said making love on a plane was easy was a fool. It was goddamn difficult, especially when the flight attendant flitted up and down the aisle every ten minutes. So they contented themselves with the sticky fondlings of first experience. And it was erotic to say the least. It was also fun. And it was a long time since either of them could remember sex being fun.

'When I get you to London, Mrs Khaled, I want time, space, and the luxury of a bed,' Nico whispered. His fingers were on her thigh, travelling up, sneaking under the leg of her panties.

Fontaine's hand fiddled with the zipper on his trousers. She could feel his maleness through the silk of his undershorts, and it was turning her on with a vengeance. 'Oh, yes, Mr Constantine, I think that can be arranged,' she murmured.

The flight attendant passed by, brisk and efficient. Could she see what was going on? They both remained stock still.

'I want to see your body,' Nico whispered. 'I know you must have a very beautiful body.'

Fontaine traced the line of his mouth with her tongue. 'None of your bullshit lines please, Nico. None of your stock phrases. You don't have to play the perfect gentleman with me. We're both grown ups.'

She had him figured out pretty quickly. He liked that. 'I want to fuck you,' he muttered. 'I want to fuck your beautiful body.' Christ! He hadn't felt free enough to talk to a woman like that since Lise Maria. Fontaine was right, when he opened his mouth out poured the perfect-gentleman bullshit.

'That's better,' Fontaine sighed. 'I have to feel you're talking to me, not doing your number.'

Their tongues played sensuous games. Then dawn and light started to filter through the windows, and it was time to stop playing and brush out clothes and adjust things.

The flight attendant served them breakfast with a thin smile. She had seen what was going on and frankly she was jealous. It wasn't like she hadn't seen it all before. But a man like Nico Constantine, well, if he hadn't been stuck next to that Khaled bitch there might have been a chance for her.

Fontaine nibbled on a slice of toast, sipped the awful coffee, and smiled at Nico. 'That was—'

He put a finger to her lips. 'And don't you go giving me any of *your* bullshit lines.'

'But it was,' she demurred.

'Agreed.'

They grinned at each other stupidly.

'I'd better go and get myself together,' Fontaine said at last. 'A quick make-up job, and my hair needs mouth to mouth resuscitation!'

It wasn't until she was gone that Nico suddenly remembered the real reason he had struck up an acquaintance with her in the first place. It didn't seem so important now. But he had the ring, and it was burning a hole in his pocket. If he asked Fontaine he was sure that she wouldn't mind taking it through customs for him. Only why involve her? The best thing was to have her do it for him unknowingly.

She had taken her make-up case and left her purse. Easy. He glanced across the aisle. The dyed blonde in the striped mink coat was engrossed in conversation with a drunken writer who was en route to London to get married for the fifth time.

Nico opened the purse. Easy. A double zipped compartment into which he dropped the ring.

Fontaine returned, her hair pulled sleekly back, a subtle make-up emphasizing her perfect bones. She smiled at him. 'Hmm . . . what an enjoyable flight. Who'd have thought?'

'Ah, but the moment I spotted you—'

'No bullshit lines, remember?'

Once again they exchanged knowing smiles.

* * *

Ricky drove the large silver Rolls-Royce much too fast. Polly, enjoying an early morning joint, admonished him. 'Mrs K. sets the speed when you're driving her. Don't you forget it.'

'What's she like?' Ricky asked for the sixth time.

'Oh, you'll either like her or you'll hate her. She's a difficult lady. No in-betweens. Typical Gemini, only ever does what she wants to do, hears what she wants to hear.'

'Has she still got a lot of money?'

Polly shrugged. 'Who knows? Hobo ain't making it any more, but her old man was loaded. Look out Ricky, you nearly hit that car. You're supposed to be a chauffeur, not a racing-car driver. And don't forget, call me Miss Brand in front of her. Wouldn't do to let her know I'm screwing the hired help.'

* * *

'Mrs Khaled, welcome back to London.' Fontaine was greeted by an airport lackey paid to smooth the way for VIPs. She handed him her make-up case. 'This way, Mrs Khaled. Everything's taken care of. If I can just have your passport . . .'

She glanced around, her eyes searching for Nico. He stood at the back of a long line for foreign passports.

She waved, blew him a kiss, and swept through British passport control.

Nico was impressed. Still married to her Arab billionaire or not she knew how to do things in style. What a stroke of genius planting the ring on her. No way would customs dare to stop her.

He thought about where he would take her for dinner. It was many years since he had been in London. Annabel's was always safe, then maybe a little gambling at the Clermont, and then bed. He anticipated a stimulating evening in every way.

* * *

Fontaine feigned surprise at seeing Polly. 'So early, darling? You shouldn't have bothered.'

Polly knew that if she hadn't bothered, Fontaine would never have let her forget it.

They kissed, the usual insincere brushing of cheeks.

'You look gorgeous!' Polly exclaimed. 'Have you had a wonderful time?'

'Terrible actually. Didn't you hear about my robbery?'

They walked to the car where Ricky respectfully held the Rolls door open.

'No! How awful! What happened?'

'I was wiped out. They took everything, absolutely everything!'

'Your jewellery?'

'Not my jewellery. Thank God that was in the bank.'

Ricky shut the car door on them. So this was the famous Mrs Khaled. Really something. She made Polly look like a bit of old rope.

* * *

Nico stood in line waiting not so patiently for twenty-five minutes. It was annoying, but a fact of life when entering a foreign country.

Naturally he was detained at customs. 'You have the look of an expensive smuggler,' Lise Maria had once told him. 'Don't ever change, I love that look.'

The customs official was polite but insistent. Every one of his Vuitton suitcases was opened up and searched. For one horrible moment Nico thought they might also search him, but luck was on his side, and he did not have to suffer the indignity of a body search.

At last he was free. He hoped that Fontaine had waited for him – she had mentioned something about her car and chauffeur meeting her. When he emerged she was nowhere to be seen. Long gone. He should have known she was not the sort of woman who would wait around.

Damn. It was annoying. He wanted to recover the ring as soon as possible. What if she discovered it? The thought of her discovering the ring was not a welcome one, but he would just bluff it out and tell her the truth – not about actually stealing the ring – just about her helping him through customs with it. And a good job too, considering he had been stopped, and his luggage searched.

Fontaine would probably be amused. Still, it would be better if she didn't find the ring, which meant he had to see her as soon as possible.

He signalled a cab and directed the driver to the Dorchester Hotel.

'Cor blimey, mate,' sneered the cabbie. 'Sure you got enough bleedin' suitcases?'

Chapter Eight

Cherry's first night with Dino was a mechanical affair. He took her to his penthouse apartment atop the Forum, showed her the view, which she admired, fixed her an exotic liqueur, which she drank, played her some sensual Barry White sounds, which she enjoyed, then moved in for the kill.

'I don't make love on a first date,' Cherry said demurely, long brownish-black eyelashes fluttering over huge blue eyes.

'What?' snapped Dino. He had a hard-on that was threatening to burst the zipper on his pants.

'I like you a lot,' Cherry continued in her sweet baby-girl voice, 'and I admire you. Only I can't make love to you, it's against my principles.'

'Principles!' exclaimed Dino, perplexed. 'To hell with your goddamn principles.'

'Don't get mad,' Cherry replied, determined to hold her ground. 'You have no right to expect me to do anything I don't want to.'

He looked her over, every gorgeous inch of her, and for the first time in his life realized he was getting a turndown. He couldn't offer her a better part in the show. She didn't want to be a cocktail waitress. If he proffered money she would throw it back in his face. But his father had taught him well – every woman has her price – and every smart man should be able to find out what that price is.

'What do you want?' Dino asked, his voice thick with desire.

Cherry shook out her long blonde curls. 'Nothing,' she replied. 'However, I like being with you, and if you want I'll stay the night with you – but I won't do anything, and you must promise not to force me.'

In all his many experiences with women this was a first. Dino was even more perplexed. He was also fascinated. He was also in love.

They spent the night together. They kissed. They caressed. She stripped down to a skimpy lace chemise that would give any red-blooded male a heart attack. He put on a bathrobe over a pair of restrictive jockey shorts. He could not believe what was going on. He fell asleep with a bad gut-ache, and awoke at seven in the morning with the same nagging pain.

Cherry lay asleep beside him, yellow hair fanned out around her face, legs slightly apart, the chemise revealing merely a wisp of lacy panties.

Enough was enough. Dino rolled on top of her, ripping her panties with one hand, and freeing himself with the other. He was inside her before she even awoke.

'Dino! You promised!' Cherry was not as outraged as she might have been.

'That was last night,' he said roughly. 'Our first date. Now it's our second date and it's my turn to call the shots.'

Cherry didn't argue. She wrapped her long slinky legs around him and gave a little sigh. Nico was a marvellous man, but as he had pointed out, what kind of a future did she have with him?

Now Dino was a different matter . . .

* * *

So far so good. Everything was going according to plan.

Bernie placed a stack of chips on red and watched black come up. Roulette. What a game. Why was he even bothering?

He glanced at his watch. Two a.m. Nico should be well on his way.

He eyed one of the cocktail waitresses. It wasn't his imagination that she'd been coming on to him all night. He gestured for another scotch, and wondered if he should hit on her for a fast fuck. Then he decided against it, he had too much on his mind, and anyway sex drained his vital energies.

At that precise moment his name was paged, and he thought, *Christ! The shit has hit.*

He rushed to the phone. It was a drunken Susanna. Just what he needed in his life. Not.

'I thought you were coming up for a drinkie,' she giggled, 'or something,' she added coyly.

Hmm . . . how should he play this one? He was in enough trouble with Susanna as it was. 'I called you earlier, guess you weren't back,' he explained. 'Sorry, hon.'

'Daddy had a party.' She hiccoughed. 'Fifteen gofers, twenty hookers, and half the mob.'

The only time she put Daddy down was when she was drunk, it was then that she saw him for the egotistical mean sonofabitch he really was.

Bernie played for time. 'Sounds like fun.'

'It wasn't. It was awful.' She paused, then added in a sexy whine. 'Come on up, Bernie, for old times' sake. We can just . . . talk.'

Oh shit! What did he have to lose? Besides which, Susanna gave the best head in Hollywood. Or if there was anyone better he'd never found them.

* * *

Cherry and Dino spent the morning in bed. They talked. They investigated the possibilities of getting further involved. They would have stayed there all day if Dino's father hadn't called and demanded his presence.

'You, my angel,' Dino informed Cherry, 'have to go back to Nico's suite, collect your things, and tell him goodbye. Got it?'

At the mention of Nico's name Cherry felt a slight twinge of guilt. Surely if she was planning to stay with Dino her loyalties lay with him? Maybe she should tell him that Nico had already left. But then again she had promised Nico she would help, and of course she wouldn't want him to come to any harm.

Dino was busy getting dressed. White slacks, a black shirt, white sports jacket. Las Vegas casual.

Cherry sat up in bed, blonde hair tumbling around her shoulders. 'Dino,' she ventured shyly, 'have you ever been married?'

Dino admired his reflection in the mirror.

'Me? No, of course not,' he said.

'Why of course not?' Cherry insisted.

'Well . . . gee . . . I don't know . . .' Why hadn't he ever gotten married? Never met anyone he wanted to marry. He looked at Cherry lying in his bed. She was so . . . delectable . . . He had an urge to eat her up. His grin widened, he would do that later.

She climbed out of bed innocently unaware of his scrutiny – or so he thought.

Now this girl had what he called a body. Streamlined and golden. Soft and firm.

She walked to the bathroom door, turned, and smiled sweetly. 'I'd *like* to get married,' she said softly. 'Wouldn't you?'

* * *

Bernie did not escape Susanna's clutches until six in the morning. He staggered from her room bleary-eyed and exhausted. They had run through the whole book of emotions, plus some very wild sex.

He hurried back to Nico's suite and collapsed on the bed.

He'd obviously blown checking with Nico on the phone, but hopefully by this time, Nico was on a plane to Europe.

Now if the pretence of Nico still being in Vegas could be kept up, then all would be fine.

Bernie fell asleep fully clothed.

* * *

As Bernie was sleeping Mrs Dean Costello awoke. She felt as if someone had hit her over the head with a hammer, and she was surprised to note that she was still fully dressed.

She struggled to recollect the events of the previous evening, but she just couldn't, her brain seemed to be all fogged up.

She vaguely remembered an extremely charming gentleman, much champagne, and hadn't she won a fair amount of money?

Her winnings! She struggled to sit up, and switched on the light.

Her winnings were neatly stacked on the bedside table. Eighteen-thousand dollars if her memory served her correctly. Propped beside them was a note.

'Madame. You are a charming and gracious lady and I am sure you would help a gentleman out of trouble. I have borrowed your diamond ring – but the loan is temporary and you shall be repaid in full. I would appreciate your co-operation of not going to the police.'

Mrs Dean Costello started to laugh. Why that cocky son-of-a-bitch. The nerve. The goddamn bare-assed nerve.

Chapter Nine

The Chelsea house was looking slightly worn, Fontaine decided. The house was part of her divorce settlement – Benjamin had kept their Belgravia mansion and bought her what she considered to be a rather unimpressive abode.

It was certainly not unimpressive, considering it was a five-bedroomed, three-reception-room elegant house with a large garden. However, it was not the Belgravia mansion with the indoor swimming pool, sauna, private cinema, internal elevator and landscaped roof garden that Fontaine was used to.

She'd furnished her new house in a hurry before she'd left for New York, and it had style. The trouble was that nobody had been living there except Mrs

Walters, her ancient and faithful housekeeper, and the rooms smelt musty and unused, there was even the faint aroma of cat pee.

'Christ!' Fontaine exclaimed. 'Why the hell didn't someone air this place? And why aren't there any fresh flowers?'

Polly shrugged. Fontaine's domestic arrangements were not her affair.

'Mrs Walters!' Fontaine yelled.

The old woman came running from the kitchen. 'Welcome home, Mrs Khaled—' she started to say.

Fontaine cut her short with a barrage of complaints.

Ricky came through the front door carrying several suitcases.

Polly winked at him. He frowned.

'I never said she was easy to work for,' Polly murmured as he passed her by.

*　*　*

Nico checked into the Dorchester and requested a suite. He was shown to a smallish suite overlooking the back. He handed the porter a hefty tip and said, 'Stay here a minute.' Then he picked up the phone and asked to see the manager immediately.

The manager was with him ten minutes later, a thin harassed man whose main concern at that moment was whether he could prevent the entire kitchen staff from walking out. Earlier in the day he had fired an assistant chef who had been caught stealing steaks – handing them to an accomplice as he took out the garbage. This had resulted in a flat statement from the rest of the kitchen workers that either the thief stayed or they walked. What to do? Mr Graheme had still not decided.

'Yes, sir, what can I do for you?' he said to Nico, experiencing major stress.

Nico gestured at his surroundings, 'Nice,' he said warmly. 'Very comfortable.' He moved over to Mr Graheme and offered him a cigar, then he put his arm conspiratorially around his shoulders. 'Mr Graheme. I stay at your hotel for the first time. The place has been highly recommended to me by many of my friends in Beverly Hills. But really, a suite like this for a man like me? Perhaps I should try the Connaught.'

Fifteen minutes later Nico was ensconced in one of the best suites in the hotel.

Mr Graheme knew a big spender when he saw one.

* * *

Once rid of Polly, Fontaine couldn't wait to get on the phone to Vanessa Grant, her closest friend in London.

'I'm back,' she announced dramatically, 'exhausted and destroyed. I can't wait to see you. How about dinner tonight?'

Vanessa hesitated, she and her husband Leonard already had dinner plans, but once Fontaine wanted something it really wasn't worth it to argue.

'I think that will be fine,' she said.

'Fine!' Fontaine snorted. 'Bloody enthusiastic welcome that is!'

'We weren't expecting you until next week.'

'I know, I know. I had to change my plans because of my robbery.'

'What robbery?'

'Darling, haven't you heard? It's all over the papers in New York.'

They chatted some more, arranging where and when to meet, then casually Fontaine asked, 'By the way, do you and Leonard know a man called Nico Constantine? An Americanized Greek. Lives in Beverly Hills, I think.'

'No, I don't think that name rings any bells. Who is he? Another of your juvenile delinquents?'

'Hardly juvenile, rather more mature.'

Vanessa laughed. 'Doesn't sound like you at all. Is he rich?'

'I'm not sure,' Fontaine said thoughtfully. 'Maybe.'

'Are you bringing him tonight?'

'Certainly not. I have a rather divine Italian count who's flying in especially to see me.'

Vanessa sighed, she had been married for too many years and had too many children. 'Sometimes I envy you,' she said wistfully.

'I know,' replied Fontaine crisply. 'If you're a good girl I'll throw him your way when I'm finished with him. He's twenty-six years old and horny as a rutting dog!'

* * *

It occurred to Nico that he had no idea how to get in touch with Fontaine. He had been so sure that she would wait for him at the airport that he had not even bothered to find out her phone number. Stupid really. But usually women waited, and after their undeniably erotic encounter on the plane he'd felt sure that Fontaine would not go rushing off. Well, hardly rushing, between passport control and customs it had taken him an hour to emerge. But still, she could at least have left a message.

He called the reception desk, told the concierge her name, and asked him to find out her phone number and address immediately.

Half an hour later the concierge gave him Benjamin Al Khaled's London office number, and a frosty secretary there said she could not possibly reveal the previous Mrs Khaled's phone number or address, and if he wished to contact her he should write in and his communication would be forwarded. Nico turned on his telephone charm, not as potent as the real thing, but effective enough to get him the number with a little gentle persuasion.

He phoned Fontaine immediately. A housekeeper answered his call and said that Mrs Khaled was resting and could not be disturbed.

He left his name and number and a message for her to call him back. Then he contacted the hotel florist and sent her three dozen red roses with a card saying, 'The flight was memorable – when do we come in for landing? Nico.'

Next he phoned Hal, Bernie's London friend, whom he had never met, but who apparently knew everyone and everything and would be able to take excellent care of the ring situation – once he had it back of course.

They arranged to meet in the bar later.

Nico then called for the valet. Time to get his personal grooming in order. It would never do to look anything but perfect.

* * *

Fontaine slept all day. At seven o'clock Mrs Walters woke her, and she got up and started her numerous preparations for the evening's activities.

'A Mr Constantine phoned,' Mrs Walters informed her. 'Also Count Paulo Rispollo. They would both like you to phone them back.' Mrs Walters busied herself with running Fontaine's bath. She had worked for her for over ten years and felt she understood her although Fontaine was extremely difficult to work for, what with her sudden screaming fits and unreasonable demands.

'Call the count back, tell him to collect me at nine o'clock.' Fontaine handed Mrs Walters a number. 'And if Mr Constantine phones again you can say I'm out.'

'They both sent flowers,' Mrs Walters continued. 'Three dozen roses from Mr Constantine. A bowl of orchids from Count Rispollo. I told the new chauffeur to be back at eight sharp, shall I send him to pick the count up?'

'I suppose so.' Fontaine stripped off her thin silk dressing gown and stretched her deliciously naked body. 'I don't think for one moment he has his own.'

Mrs Walters scurried off, not happy to view her employers nudity. Fontaine climbed into a her hot bath.

Count Paulo Rispollo. Young. Good-looking. Unfortunately he didn't have a pot to piss in. But he adored her. He'd met her in New York and declared undying love. Probably bi-sexual, but very passable in bed, and that's where it all mattered, wasn't it? Besides, it was good for her image, a young handsome escort, especially a titled one.

She thought briefly of Nico Constantine, then put the thought quickly aside. Trouble. She sensed it. And anyway, since when did she date men older than herself? What a positively boring idea. Who needed real conversations? All she needed was a fine young body – no complications – just sex. And if sometimes she had to pick up the bills, well, that was life.

* * *

Nico was irritated when Fontaine failed to return his call by the time he met up with Hal. He was more than irritated, he needed to recover the ring urgently.

Hal turned out to be an amiable fortyish American promoter operating out of London. Attractive, if you liked the Dean Martin gone-to-seed type. Constantly stoned and well dressed, his specialty was hustling elderly widows.

He greeted Nico warmly, asked after Bernie, and said, 'Where's the item? I have a set up waiting to accept. I'm working on a split percentage, does that suit you?'

'Sure, but I have a problem,' Nico explained. 'I

met a woman on the plane. I thought it would be safer for her to bring the ring in. I don't have it back yet.'

Hal made a face. 'I was given to understand time was of the essence.'

'It is, it is,' Nico said quickly. 'I'm trying to reach the woman. Her name is Fontaine Khaled.'

Hal let out a low whistle. 'The ice queen herself! Is she back?'

'You know her?'

Hal laughed. 'Sure I know her. She owns Hobo. My good friend Tony Blake used to run it for her – along with a few more personal services. He's living in L.A. now trying to recover from the experience. What the hell was she doing with you? You're a little over her age limit.'

'What the hell was *I* doing with her?' Nico retorted quickly. 'She's a little over mine.'

'Does she know about the ring?' Hal asked.

'No. I concealed it in her purse. I've been trying to contact her.'

'Don't worry. We'll run into her tonight. The first place she'll go is Hobo, and *we'll* be there to greet her.'

* * *

109

'What you need is another Tony,' Vanessa whispered. 'Franco just doesn't have it where it counts.'

Fontaine glanced around the half-empty restaurant at Hobo. She hardly knew any of the people who were there – a dreary-looking bunch of bores.

'Do *you* know who any of these people are?' she asked Vanessa.

'Absolutely not,' Vanessa replied. 'It seems anyone can get in nowadays. Now when Tony was here he kept it tight, if you know what I mean.'

'For Christ's sake, do shut up about Tony. I know you had the hots for him, but he's long gone. He got a little too big for his Gucci's.'

'Or something!' giggled Vanessa.

'Quite,' agreed Fontaine. She glanced around the restaurant again. It was annoying, but unfortunately true, Hobo was no longer the place to be seen. Franco had let things go.

Count Paulo seemed to be enjoying every minute. His boyish face glowed with the thrill of being out with the glorious Fontaine Khaled. He watched her admiringly. Leonard, Vanessa's husband, tried to involve him in a business dialogue, but Paulo was more interested in gazing at his date.

Fontaine impatiently tapped long scarlet fingernails on the table. 'Why don't we move on?' she suggested. 'Where is everyone going now?'

'There's a divine new club called Dickies,' Vanessa

enthused. 'Gay, of course – well, more mixed really. The waiters wear satin shorts and run around on roller skates. They serve *the* most decadent drinks, you'll be drunk for a week!'

'Let's go,' said Fontaine. 'I suppose I should see where the real action is.'

She rose from the table and swept out of the restaurant.

Franco snapped to attention. 'Mrs Khaled, you ees leaving us so early. Something the matter?'

'Yes, Franco,' her voice was cold. 'You, as it happens. You're fired.'

* * *

Hal produced two beautiful girls. A mixed-race croupier on a two-week vacation, and a streaked blonde who was into meditation. Nico got the blonde, although he insisted to Hal he didn't want a date.

'It'll look better,' Hal explained. 'Trust me, I know Fontaine. Besides, tonight is my night off. Once a week I treat myself to a broad under sixty.'

'So have two,' Nico suggested. 'I don't want one.'

They arrived at Hobo ten minutes after Fontaine had left.

'Mrs Khaled around?' Hal asked Franco.

'She come, she go.' Franco replied, then he burst

into a stream of Italian abuse about his soon-to-be-former employer.

'Nobody ever called Fontaine a pussycat,' Hal said, agreeing.

'A *beetch*!' Franco shrieked. 'I work my ass to the bone, and like that – poof – she throw me out.'

'Yeah,' said Hal. 'Like Tony. Remember Tony? You took his job.'

Franco glared.

'Come on,' Hal said to Nico. 'Knowing our Fontaine, she's checking out the competition.'

* * *

Fontaine was indeed checking out the competition, and she could see immediately why Dickies had taken over. The music was great, the waiters outrageous, and the whole ambience reminded her of Hobo when it had first opened. Her kaleidoscope eyes surveyed the scene. Yes, all the same old faces. Every one of the Hobo regulars.

'Fun, isn't it?' Vanessa enthused.

'Hmmm . . . Not bad.' Fontaine turned to Count Paulo. 'Let's dance.'

The dance floor was crowded – unlike the barren expanse at Hobo. As Fontaine moved her body expertly in time to Beyonce, her mind was racing. What Hobo needed was a revamp. New lighting. A change of menu. Definitely a different disc jockey. And a manager with the charisma Tony had possessed.

The music changed to a slow ballad.

Count Paulo pulled her close. Funny, but she didn't fancy him one little bit. He just seemed boring.

'Fontaine, gorgeous! When did you get back?' Suddenly she was the centre of attention – so-called friends greeting her on all sides.

She smiled and nodded enjoying the scrutiny. She was no fool. She knew what they were all thinking: poor old Fontaine. No more billionaire husband; no more successful club. What was she going to do? Well, she bloody well wasn't going to do what they all wanted – fade away defeated. She was back with a vengeance, and they'd better all believe it.

'Hello, darlin', what you doin' here? Hobo not the same since you threw Tony out?'

She turned to confront the owner of the raucous Cockney accent. It was Sammy, a small wiry-haired dress manufacturer who only went out with girls under the age of sixteen.

She gave him a frosty smile. 'I'll find another Tony,' she said coolly. 'He was never an original.'

'Oh, yeah?' Sammy winked knowingly. 'What you need is a guy like me to run the place for you. I'd soon get it all back together 'ave 'em raving in the aisles in no time. Wanna gimme a try?'

Fontaine looked him over with a mixture of amusement and contempt. 'You?' The one word said it all.

'All right, all right, I know when I'm not appreciated,' Sammy said, backing off.

Count Paulo rubbed her thighs. 'Who was that?' he asked possessively.

'Do you have to hold me so tight?' Her voice was ice. 'You're creasing my dress.'

* * *

Nico noticed Fontaine immediately. Well, she could hardly be missed. She certainly was a striking woman.

He watched her on the dance floor clutched in the arms of some young stud. She obviously had a predilection for young studs – just as he had for fresh-faced young beauties.

'Told you she'd be here,' Hal announced triumphantly.

'Can we dance, Nico?' One of the girls started pulling on his jacket sleeve. 'Hal won't mind, he doesn't dance.'

Nico gently removed her tugging hand and adjusted his sleeve. 'Not right now, dear.'

Hal spotted his friend Sammy, and moved over to join him and his teenage companion.

After introductions, Hal explained to Sammy that Nico wanted to get together with Fontaine.

Sammy roared with laughter. 'You gotta be kidding. No chance, her highness wouldn't sniff in your direction!'

'Really?' Nico said, heading confidently toward the dance floor. 'Just watch her sniff!'

Chapter Ten

In Las Vegas, Bernie Darrell began to realize that protecting Nico was not exactly going to do him any good. Okay, so he was on fairly friendly terms with Dino Fonicetti, and he knew the father and the brother to nod to. But they were hard people, they had their reputation to consider, and when the fact that Nico had skipped town owing five-hundred-and-fifty-thousand grand was revealed, and then it came out that he, Bernie, had helped in the deception, well, that wouldn't be good.

By Tuesday evening he was apprehensive. And when Cherry baby came knocking at the door to pick up her things, he was even more so.

'I shall have to tell Dino that Nico has left,' Cherry announced. 'I refuse to lie.'

Bernie was startled. 'What the hell you talking about?' he snapped. 'We're helping Nico, remember?'

'I have a certain loyalty to Dino,' Cherry replied, her expression stubborn.

'Loyalty? To Dino?' Bernie was amazed. 'What the fuck you talking about?'

Cherry was oblivious to his anger as she packed up the few things she had brought with her. 'Of course, I won't mention that Nico left last night, I'll just say he's gone—'

Bernie grabbed her wrist roughly. 'You'll do no such fucking thing!'

'You're hurting me.' Cherry's blue eyes filled with tears. 'I'll tell Dino.'

Bernie released her. 'I don't believe this! I don't fuckin' believe it!' He mimicked her voice – '"I'll tell Dino." What is this, love's young dream all of a sudden? A one-night screw and the blonde and the hood are star-crossed lovers?'

Cherry raised her voice for the first time since Bernie had known her. 'It is possible, you know, for two people to fall in love. Dino is a warm and kind human being—'

'Holy shit!'

'We're going to get married if you must know.'

'I need a drink.' Bernie walked to the mini-bar and fixed himself a large scotch. His mind was racing. This was some situation. It could only happen to him. One moment the dumb cunt was trailing Nico to Las Vegas determined to sort out their future together. The next – true love with a Mafioso-one-night stand. Unbelievable!

He tried to soften his voice. 'Hey, Cherry – I'm pleased for you and Dino, really I am. But if you tell him Nico has split, we're all in trouble, you included.'

'Not me,' Cherry protested indignantly. 'It wasn't *my* idea!'

'Yes, you, baby,' Bernie insisted. 'How do you think your future bridegroom is going to feel when I tell him last night was a setup?'

Cherry's eyes widened. 'What do you mean?'

'You spent the night with Dino so that Nico could get out of town. Right?'

'I suppose so . . .' she said reluctantly.

'Don't suppose. It's a fact of life. Now if Dino finds that out he is not going to be exactly thrilled.' Bernie took a deep breath. 'So listen carefully. You know nothing. Nico was here today when you picked up your things. You told him goodbye, that's all you know. And as far as you're concerned he's still here.'

'But I still think—'

'Listen to me, sweetheart. Listen and learn. If your future plans include being Mrs Fonicetti, play it my way. You tell Dino the truth, and who knows how he'll react. Personally I wouldn't want to risk it.'

Cherry frowned. Bernie did have a point. 'Well, all

right,' she said hesitantly. 'But when will Dino find out that Nico has gone?'

Bernie poured himself another scotch. 'By the time he finds out, Nico will be back, so don't you worry your pretty little head about it.'

Cherry nodded. 'Okay, Bernie, if you say so.'

So far so good. But could she be trusted? She was such a fucking idiot. Bernie sighed. How the hell had he ever gotten involved in this whole caper? Here he was – stuck in Las Vegas. What about his business? He had meetings to attend, and it would be at least a couple of days before Nico returned. That is if all went according to plan.

Cherry was packed and ready to go. She smiled sweetly at him and stuck out a small delicate hand.

'Goodbye, Bernie,' she said. 'And thank you for everything.'

Christ! She sounded like she'd taken a course in good manners!

'Yeah, well, I won't be leaving yet, so I guess we'll be seeing each other around. Now don't forget what I told you. Be a smart girl and you'll go far.'

Cherry departed.

Bernie made a few mental calculations. Nico should be arriving in London about now. Hal had been alerted to the situation. If all went smoothly the ring would be sold and the money in Nico's pocket within twenty-four hours. Nico would get on a plane immediately and be back in the suite before anyone realized he was gone. Pay off his markers. Back to L.A. Mission accomplished. No broken bones.

It sounded easy.

Bernie wished the whole goddamn caper was over and done with.

Chapter Eleven

'Mrs Khaled.' Nico cut in on the dance floor, subtly elbowing Count Paulo aside. 'What a pleasure to see you again so soon.'

'What do you think you are doing!' Count Paulo exploded. 'You cannot—'

'It's all right, Paulo.' Fontaine waved him aside. 'Run along and sit down, I'll join you in a minute.'

The count glared at Nico before reluctantly departing.

Nico took her in his arms, even though the beat was strident disco.

'Nice-looking boy,' Nico remarked. 'Similar to the one I saw you with at Kennedy airport.'

'Yes,' Fontaine drawled. 'I like them full of energy.'

Nico raised an eyebrow.

Fontaine gave a husky laugh.

'Did you get my flowers?' he asked.

'Very nice. How did you find my address?'

'If I want something I usually manage to get it.'

'Oh, really? We're so alike.'

'Thanks for waiting at the airport,' he said. 'That was thoughtful of you.'

'I'm hardly a taxi service.'

'I was under the impression we had a date.'

'A date?' She laughed derisively. 'How delightfully old world of you.'

'Has anybody ever told you that you're a bitch?'

'Frequently,' she responded.

Nico pulled her in very close indeed. Count Paulo, skulking at the edge of the dance floor continued to glare.

'Well, Mrs Khaled,' Nico said softly, 'are we going to finish what we started on the plane?'

Fontaine responded to his maleness. 'Why not, Mr Constantine.' She sighed. 'Why not indeed?'

* * *

'Bleedin' hell!' Sammy exclaimed, as they all watched Nico and Fontaine exit. ''E's only done it! What's 'e got? Mink-lined balls!'

'Oh, Sammy, you are *awful*!' his teenage girlfriend squealed.

'The guy has a lot of charm,' Hal stated. 'Not to mention the best tailor I've ever seen.'

'Charm schmarm – all Fontaine wants to know about is the size of the bank balance or the cock!'

'Honestly, Sammy!'

'It's all right darlin' – you'll be OK on both counts!'

* * *

'I do believe she's leaving,' Vanessa whispered to Leonard.

'I think you're right,' he replied.

'Absolutely charming.' Vanessa sniffed. 'You'd think she'd have the manners to say goodnight.'

'Nobody ever accused Fontaine of having any manners,' Leonard pointed out. 'Who is that man anyway?'

Vanessa peered at the couple as they left the dance floor.

'I don't know. He doesn't look her style at all, too mature, but definitely attractive.'

'Rich, I suppose,' Leonard said brusquely.

'I suppose,' Vanessa agreed.

'God!' Leonard exclaimed, 'Don't tell me we're stuck with her Italian juvenile.'

'Looks like we are.' Vanessa said, watching as a surly Count Paulo approached. Oh yes. There was certainly something to be said for the young ones. Maybe if Fontaine had finished with him . . .

Vanessa wasn't proud. She had accepted seconds from her friend before.

*   *   *

Ricky tried to concentrate on his driving, but it wasn't easy. God Almighty, you would think he had a couple of teenage ravers in the back. He attempted to keep his eye on what was happening in the rear-view mirror. Naturally Mrs Khaled had pressed the button which sent the glass partition up, cutting him off from their sounds.

He drove the Rolls-Royce slower than usual, until Fontaine lowered the glass partition an inch and snapped, 'Do hurry up, Ricky.'

Bitch!

He hoped he'd be free after he'd dropped Fontaine at her house. He was feeling very randy, and he wondered if Polly would be up. Better than sleeping the night in that pisshole of a room he'd rented.

The Rolls glided up to Fontaine's house. Ricky jumped out and opened the car door for them. He gazed disinterestedly off into space.

'Will you be needing me again tonight, Mrs Khaled?' he ventured.

'No, Ricky.' Her voice was light and full of excitement. 'Tonight I will not be needing you.'

'What time tomorrow, Mrs Khaled?'

'Ten o'clock – I'd like you here every morning at ten.'

'Yes, Mrs Khaled.'

He waited until they turned to walk into the house, before glancing at his watch. It was already two in the morning. Some job. It was a good thing the wages were right. He wondered what had happened to the Italian ice cream. Must have got himself dumped . . . Ricky couldn't help smiling. He liked a woman who behaved like a man.

* * *

It was an erotic experience.

It was clothes off on the stairs.

It was hot tongues and warm bodies.

It was touch – feel – smell.

Fontaine felt herself out of control for once. Here was a man she didn't have to tell what she wanted. Nico knew everything. He was very accomplished.

'You're like a dancer,' Nico breathed in her ear. 'You make love like a dancer who has been in training.'

'Hmmm, and you, you're like a stallion . . .'

He laughed. 'The Greek Stallion. It sounds like a

bad movie! When I was twenty I was a stallion, now I know what I'm doing.'

'You certainly do!' Fontaine sighed.

They made love endlessly, or so it seemed to both of them. They were comfortable together, there was none of the awkwardness that sometimes happens the first time two people are in bed together.

The added bonus was that they could talk, not about anything special, just conversation.

Fontaine never had conversations with her transient studs, sometimes verbal skirmishes, but never conversations.

The same applied to Nico and his fresh-faced beauties. How boring and bland they all seemed once the initial thrill of a new body was over.

The thing that turned him on about Fontaine more than anything was her mind. She might be one tough lady, but she had wit and perception, and he wanted to dig deeper and find out more about the woman beneath the sophisticated veneer.

'I want to know all about you,' he ventured. 'Everything, from the beginning.'

Fontaine rolled over in bed. She felt delightfully satisfied. '*You're* the man of mystery. I meet you on a plane, the next minute we're in bed. And all I know about you is your name. You could be—'

'What?' He pinned her arms to the bed playfully. 'A mass murderer? A maniac?' He kissed her hard and released her. 'And don't tell me Mrs Khaled hasn't gone to bed with a man she met on a plane before.'

'Well.' She laughed softly. 'Perhaps once or twice.'

'Ah, yes, once or twice, I bet.' He smiled. 'How many men *have* you had?'

Fontaine stretched and got out of bed. 'Let's put it this way, Nico, a meal a day means one never goes hungry.'

'Come back here,' he joked. 'I want my dessert!'

'I'm about to take a shower, I need reviving. Why don't you go downstairs and bring up a bottle of Grand Marnier, I'll show you a delicious new way to drink it.' She went into the bathroom and closed the door.

Nico lay back still smiling. He felt completely relaxed. Then he remembered the ring. Wasn't that the reason he was here? Well, originally . . .

He could hear water running in the bathroom. He got off the bed and looked around the room for the purse Fontaine had carried on the plane. He couldn't see it, but the mirrored door of a large walk-in closet stood invitingly open. He peered inside. Racks and racks of shoes stacked in neat rows. Shelves for sweaters, shirts, T-shirts, scarves, gloves. Belts and beads hanging in rows. Expensive lingerie in Perspex drawers. And handbags. All on a bottom shelf. About twenty-five of them.

He looked through them quickly, searching for the Gucci stripe. There were five with Gucci stripes, but none were the right one.

He swore softly under his breath, then suddenly saw the one he was looking for. It was hanging on the back of the door.

He grabbed it quickly, unzipped the side compartment, and there, nestled at the bottom, was his ring.

Fontaine appeared exactly at the wrong moment, a pink towel wrapped around her sarong style. Her voice was icy, 'What exactly do you think you are doing?'

Nico jumped. He felt like a schoolboy caught with his hand inside the cookie jar. He wished he had put his pants on at least. There is nothing more daunting for a man than to be caught in an awkward situation with a limp dick hanging down.

'Well?' Fontaine could make one word a meal.

Nico smiled. Charm. His smile had got him through many tricky situations. 'You're never going to believe this,' he said.

'Try me.' Her glacial expression did not crack.

'Well . . .' he tried to edge past her.

She blocked his way.

'It's a long story,' he said quickly. 'I'm sure it will amuse you. Let me put some clothes on and I'll tell you.'

Patiently, calmly, Fontaine interrupted him. 'No,'

she said sharply. 'Just tell me what you were doing in my purse, and show me what you have in your hand. Now, Nico, right now. I don't want to hear any amusing stories, I'm not in the mood for a good laugh.'

Nico shrugged. 'I can assure you I'm not taking anything of yours.'

'I can assure you of that too.'

'I had this ring, I thought maybe I would have problems with customs.'

He opened his hand and showed her the diamond.

She glanced at it briefly, then at him.

'I was going to ask you if you would mind bringing it through for me, but I didn't know you that well. Of course, I was going to tell you—'

'You bastard,' she said, her voice an icy blast. 'You son-of-a-bitch nasty little hustler. You used me on the plane this evening. How dare you!'

'I only—'

She held up an imperious hand. 'I do not want to hear. I want you out of my house and my life. Immediately.'

'But Fontaine . . .'

She wasn't listening. She was gathering his clothes together, which she then threw at him. 'Out!' she snapped. 'Before I have you thrown out.'

'I think we should talk about it.'

'Why? What more do you want from me? You've

fucked me every way you can. And I might add that the screwing I got in bed wasn't half as good as the screwing I *really* got from you. So go. Now!'

She walked back into her bathroom and slammed the door.

Quickly Nico dressed. There was no point in staying around to argue. After all, he had what he'd come for. It was time to go.

And so he did. Reluctantly.

Chapter Twelve

'What?' Joseph Fonicetti regarded his youngest son through narrowed eyes. 'What the fuck did I hear you say?'

Dino shuffled his feet uneasily. How come everywhere he was king, yet in front of his father he was zero, nothing, a goddamned kid again.

'I . . . I . . . er . . . well . . . I'm gonna get married.'

Joseph threw him a long unnerving stare. 'Just like that. Out of the blue you've found yourself a girl fit to be your wife. In Vegas you've found a girl to take the Fonicetti name. Who is this beauty? A showgirl? A cocktail waitress? A hooker?' Joseph spat his disgust into a handy ashtray.

'She's a very lovely girl,' Dino said quickly. 'Not from Las Vegas.'

'None of them are from here, they only come here to develop their cunts and their bankrolls!'

'She's a nice girl,' Dino said defensively. 'You'll love her.'

Joseph shut his eyes and mulled over the fact that Dino was a good-looking boy, but when it came to women he was dense. Now David, his older son, was smart. He had a wife, a plain Italian girl who would never give him a moment's trouble, and he fucked around with Las Vegas gash on his terms only.

'When did you meet this girl?' Joseph asked. 'A month? Two months ago? How come I've never heard you mention her before?'

'Cherry only got here this week,' Dino said defensively. 'You know how it is, this is the girl I want to marry. It happened just like that.'

Yes. Joseph knew how it was. Some smart broad had hooked her little finger round Dino's cock and thought she was going to get lucky. Well, she could think again. When Joseph was ready for Dino to get married – he personally would arrange it. A selection of Italian virgins would be shipped in, just as they'd been for David, and Dino could take his pick.

'So, this Cherry. Who'd she come here with?'

Dino answered quickly. He wanted to lie, but his father would find out the truth he always did. 'She came here with Bernie Darrell, they're friends, nothing more.'

134

'Sure,' Joseph sneered. 'Bernie Darrell brought a girl all the way to Vegas and they're just friends. I believe that. Who wouldn't?'

'She came here to see Nico Constantine, then she met me. Neither of us expected this, it kinda just happened.'

'And what did Nico do? Kiss you both and wish you luck?'

'She and Nico, it was over.'

Joseph nodded. 'I guess, she wasn't influenced by the fact that Nico was losing his ass at the tables. By the way, have you made arrangements with him about paying?'

'I will, Dad, I will.' Dino said quickly.

'Sure, leave it go while you make wedding arrangements. Who cares about the money?'

'Nico's good for it.'

'He'd better be.'

'He is. I'll deal with it today.' Dino coughed nervously. 'About Cherry. When can I bring her to meet you?'

Joseph nodded thoughtfully, he had an idea. 'Tonight,' he said, 'we'll have dinner, the whole family. We'll discuss your wedding.'

Dino was relieved. It seemed his father was accepting Cherry without too much of a fight. He must have realized it was no use fighting. After all, he, Dino, was not exactly David who could be forced into a dull marriage with a placid Italian lump.

Dino gave a relieved smile. His family would all love Cherry. From the moment Joseph met her it would be totally cool.

* * *

'We have an invitation,' Susanna said, sitting down and joining Bernie at a table in the coffee shop.

'We do?' He was halfway through a prune danish, wondering if it would solve his bowel problem.

'Yup.' Susanna studied the menu. 'Daddy wants us to have dinner with him and the Fonicettis tonight. I accepted on our behalf.'

'You did?' Bernie wondered how they had become a pair again. Two nights of torrid love-making and the divorce was supposed to be a past memory?

'He's invited Nico Constantine too. Will you tell him? I can't get an answer from his suite.'

Bernie nearly choked on his danish. 'Why Nico?'

'Why not?' Susanna said. 'Daddy likes him.'

Yes, and hates me, Bernie thought. The last time they'd met had been just before the divorce. Carlos Brent had confronted him in the Beverly Hills Hotel Polo lounge.

'You dumbass bastard,' Carlos had growled. 'All I need is the word from Susanna, and my boys' club will be playing catch with your balls. You're lucky she's not vindictive.'

Nice! They had not spoken nor run into each other since.

'I don't know if Nico will make it,' Bernie hedged. 'He's gotten very involved with a girl here.'

'What girl?' Susanna demanded.

'Some chick, I don't know her name.'

'He can bring a date, it'll be okay.'

'I'll try to reach him.'

Susanna yawned and giggled. 'Can you believe what's happened to us? Can you believe it, Bernie? My analyst will have a blue fit!'

To be truthful Bernie was finding it very hard to believe himself. One moment he and Susanna were the worst of enemies, the next they were making love like randy soldiers on twenty-four-hour leave! He had to admit that for him she was the absolute greatest in bed, but a pain in the ass to live with. Unfortunately Carlos had spoiled the pants off her.

A chubby waitress came rushing over. 'Miss Brent,' she gushed, 'what can I get for you today?'

Miss Brent. It had always been Miss Brent, never ever Mrs Darrell. And on a couple of memorable occasions – memorable because of the blazing fight that followed – he'd even been addressed as Mr Brent.

'I dunno, Maggi,' Susanna said, she knew all of the elderly waitresses by name since she'd been coming to the hotel her entire life. 'I think maybe a cheese danish and a black coffee.'

Maggi beamed. 'Certainly, dear.'

'I was thinking,' Susanna said, turning to Bernie. 'Why don't you and Nico fly back to L.A. with me? I can use Daddy's plane whenever I want. I thought maybe tomorrow. You could stay at the house, Starr would like that.'

Starr was their very cute four-year-old daughter. She was also Carlos Brent's only grandchild, and as such she was spoiled rotten, just like her mother.

'I don't know,' Bernie answered, his mind racing. 'I promised Nico I'd stay with him.'

Susanna shot him a dirty look. 'Whose hand would you sooner hold? Mine or Nico's?'

'Yours, of course.'

'Anyway, his new girlfriend seems to be doing a pretty good job of holding his. I haven't even seen him yet.'

'You know how it is.'

'I certainly do.' She pushed her tinted shades up into her hair and sighed. 'We must have been mad to have gotten divorced. Why did we do it?'

Did she really expect an answer?

Because you nagged the shit out of me, Susanna.

Because you required my balls to be your balls.

Because Daddy, Daddy, Daddy is enough to drive anyone to divorce.

Bernie shrugged. 'I don't know.'

Susanna giggled, that 'I wanna get laid' look came

into her eyes. 'Why don't we forget about lunch?' she suggested. 'Why don't we just toddle upstairs and smoke some grass.'

'Yeah, why not?' he said, thinking that he certainly had nothing else to do with his time while he waited for Nico to surface.

Chapter Thirteen

'Who was he?' asked Vanessa over the phone.

'Some boring con artist,' snapped Fontaine.

'He didn't look little to me, rather Omar Sharif actually.'

'A poor imitation.'

'You certainly left in a hurry, Paulo was furious.'

'Look, darling, I have to go, got a million things to do. I'll call you later.'

'Don't forget the fashion lunch tomorrow,' Vanessa reminded her.

'I've written it in my book,' Fontaine said, putting the phone down, and checking out her appearance in the mirror. Chic, but understated. Silk shirt, pleated skirt, Valentino jacket. Just the outfit to interview aspiring managers for Hobo. She had phoned Polly first thing and given her a blast. 'Get me some young, attractive, would-be front men. Franco's the reason Hobo is down the drain. Find me another Tony. I'll be over to see what you have at four o'clock.'

* * *

Polly hung up the phone and snuggled up to Ricky. 'You'd better move your butt,' she said. 'Mrs K. is up early and raring to get goin'.'

'She told me ten o'clock,' Ricky replied.

'In that case, we might just have time. Oh crap! I forgot. I'm the one with the early appointment.' She bounced out of bed. 'Any ideas how I go about finding a tall sexy man with a big dick?'

Ricky laughed crudely. 'Don't I fit that bill?'

'Yes, you do. Only you got the chauffeur's job, and Mrs K. would never understand a change of image midstream.'

'Why not? She seems like a pretty smart lady to me.'

'Really?' Polly winked. 'Fancy her already, do you?'

Ricky laughed. 'Wouldn't mind dipping my toe in.'

'She'd want more than your toe, sonny. Much more . . .'

'Why don't you come over here an' shut up.'

Every time he thought about his employer he found himself getting quite randy.

* * *

With the ring back in his possession Nico felt more secure. The delay had not been planned, and he imagined that Bernie must be worried by his silence. They had arranged that they would not make contact until he had actually fenced the ring and was on his way back to Vegas. But still, maybe he should call, put Bernie's mind at rest. Then again, maybe not. Didn't want to alarm him unnecessarily. If all went well, and Hal came across, he could be on a plane within hours.

He delivered the ring personally to Hal the morning after his confrontation scene with Fontaine.

Hal wasn't pleased as he groped his way to the front door of his Park Lane service flat clad in a pair of black silk pyjamas. 'Jesus Christ!' he exclaimed. 'What the frig's the time?'

Nico glanced at his watch. 'Nine forty-five. Too early for you?'

'Damn right it is. I never get up before two or three.'

'This is an emergency.'

'Yeah. I understand,' Hal said, leading the way into an unused kitchen, where he set about making coffee. 'What happened? Fontaine throw you out early? Or didn't you get to stay?'

'I didn't stay,' Nico said, not wanting to get into it.

'Wise move. Fontaine's a balls-breaker.'

'How well do you know her?'

'Well enough.'

'Did you ever—'

'Me? Are you kidding?' Hal began to laugh. 'Fontaine wouldn't glance in my direction – not that I would ever want her to. She likes 'em young. When she was married to the Arab, she used his money to set herself up in business.'

Nico produced the ring from his pocket and showed it to Hal.

Hal let out a long whistle. 'That's really something, absolutely bee-u-tiful.'

'When will I hear from you?' Nico asked. 'I gotta get back to Vegas as soon as possible.'

Hal poured water over instant coffee, already thinking of how he would spend his commission. 'A cash transaction like this, maybe some time tomorrow.'

'Christ!' Nico exclaimed. 'It has to be sooner than that.'

'I'll do my best, but there's a lot of money involved here. Be patient and relax. Go do some gambling. The London clubs are the best.'

Nico gave a hollow laugh. 'Why do you think I'm in trouble today?'

* * *

Polly and Fontaine sat together at Hobo interviewing would-be hosts. So far they had seen six, none of them suitable.

Fontaine was irritated, and getting more so by the minute. Why was it so goddamn difficult to find an attractive, ambitious, sexy, ballsy young man?

She thought briefly of Jump Jennings. Thought even more briefly of importing him. Changed her mind, and peered at the next young man in line for the job.

'Hmmm . . . Not bad.' Fontaine yawned. 'What did you think, Polly?'

'I think that the Cockney accent is just a little too much.'

Fontaine picked a nut from the glass dish on the table and tossed it into her mouth. 'Yes. I suppose you're right. Cockney was in last year, now it seems to be chinless or gay, but I still say what we need is a macho front man.'

'I know, exactly like the fabulous Tony. Right?'

Fontaine smiled dreamily. 'You never met him, did you?'

'I wish I had. But I was in America the year of

Hobo's ascent, although I certainly heard plenty about him.'

'At the beginning Tony was the very best. In every way I might add.'

'Then why did you fire him?'

'His ambitions screwed up his head.'

The next young man was better than the others. Curly black hair, tight faded jeans, a certain confidence.

Polly consulted a businesslike clipboard. 'And you are . . . ?'

'Steve Valentine.'

Fontaine and Polly exchanged quick amused looks.

'You're currently fronting a club in Ealing?' Polly asked. 'Is that right?'

'I've been the manager there for eighteen months.'

'Do you enjoy it?' Fontaine said, her kaleidoscope eyes inspecting every inch of him.

Steve stared at her. 'Yeah, well it's all right. But I'd sooner work in the West End.'

'I'm sure you would,' Fontaine said, picking up a cigarette and waiting for him to light it.

He fumbled for a cheap lighter and did the honours.

'Hmmm . . .' said Fontaine, still inspecting him. 'Do you have a girlfriend?'

Steve's stare became bold. 'One wouldn't be enough for me, Mrs Khaled.'

'I bet it wouldn't.' She turned to Polly. 'I think we should give Mr Valentine a try, don't you, Polly?'

* * *

When Nico left Hal's apartment he decided to make the most of his last day in London. He had in his possession the six-thousand dollars that Bernie had withdrawn from his office safe, and apart from his hotel bill he would have no other expenses in London. By the time Hal disposed of the ring he would have more than enough cash to pay his debts in Vegas, repay Bernie, and still have a few thousand dollars left over.

Of course, then he would have to start thinking about his future. But he would worry about that when the time came. Mrs Dean Costello must be compensated, that would be his responsibility if her insurance company had not already taken care of it. He had every intention of repaying her if she was not insured. How, he didn't quite know. But Nico had supreme confidence in his ability to deal with any situation. Plus the fact that no way would a ring like that be uninsured.

He thought about Fontaine Khaled. Flowers of course. Red roses naturally. Six dozen with a discreet note of apology. And a gift. Not the usual token trinket, something nice and substantial. Something beautiful that she would love.

Even though he would be leaving London he had every intention of seeing her again. It was not inconceivable that he might return as soon as everything was settled.

Fontaine interested him like no other woman had since Lise Maria. He knew her, and yet he also knew that he had barely scratched the surface. She was an arrogant, assured, tough woman. Underneath the veneer was the woman he really wanted to know. Vulnerable, soft, lovable, searching for the right man, just as he, unknowingly, had been searching for the right woman.

He hailed a taxi and directed the driver to Boucheron, the Bond Street jewellery store.

* * *

Ricky watched Fontaine in the rear-view mirror as the Rolls glided through heavy traffic. Her eyes were closed, legs crossed, skirt riding up to reveal stocking tops. She wore old-fashioned suspenders! Christmas! Bloody suspenders! The only place he had ever seen those were in girly magazines!

He immediately felt randy, in spite of fifteen hot sticky minutes with Polly in the morning.

'Ricky.'

He shifted his eyes quickly to his boss's face. She was awake.

148

'Yes, Mrs Khaled.'

'Did you collect my clothes from the cleaners?'

'Yes, Mrs Khaled?'

'And did you pick up my prescription?'

'Yes, Mrs Khaled.'

'Good. When we get home you can take some time off. I won't be needing you until ten tonight.'

'Thanks, Mrs Khaled.' He glanced at the clock on the dashboard. It was nearly five. He was rather bushed himself. He sneaked another look in the mirror. She had pulled her skirt down. Spoilsport.

'Oh, and Ricky,' she said coolly.

'Yes, Mrs Khaled?'

'Be a good boy and keep your eyes on the road.'

'Yes, Mrs Khaled.'

Bitch!

* * *

Nico enjoyed himself. He'd always possessed a knack for spending money. Three-thousand dollars went on a diamond-studded heart for Fontaine. Another couple of thousand on a Cartier watch for Bernie. And twelve-hundred on clothes for himself – cashmere sweaters and silk shirts from Turnbull & Asser.

Satisfied, he returned to his hotel.

Hal waited in the lobby. Things were progressing even faster than Nico had hoped.

'Good news?' he questioned.

'Let's go upstairs,' Hal replied.

They took the elevator up to Nico's suite in silence.

Once inside Hal produced the diamond ring and flung it on the bed. 'It's a fake, a fuckin' fake!' He spat in disgust. 'What the hell kind of game are you playin', Nico?'

Chapter Fourteen

Bernie was stoned. Nicely so. Just enough to be able to face Carlos Brent and the Fonicettis with a smooth smile.

He prepared to leave Susanna at six o'clock with the promise to collect her at seven.

She lay in bed, also stoned, and suggested for the sixth time that they should get married again.

'Why?' Bernie asked. 'We're having such a good time together not being married.'

'I know,' agreed Susanna. 'But for Starr's sake it would be nice.'

Not to mention Carlos, Bernie thought. *Big Daddy would be furious if he knew what was going on.*

'Don't forget to invite Nico,' Susanna called out after him.

'If he's around,' Bernie replied.

'He must be back by now. Who *is* the new girlfriend?'

'I told you, I don't know. See you later.'

Bernie made his escape and returned to the suite. It would be a bonus if Nico was waiting to greet him.

He wasn't.

Bernie tried to decide if a phone call was in order. He needed to know what was happening. How much longer could he keep up the pretence that Nico was around? Of course he couldn't risk phoning from the Forum. He would have to stroll over to Caesars or the MGM Grand and use an anonymous phone booth.

After taking a shower, he changed his clothes, then sprayed his mouth with a fresh mint breath spray, and set off to make the phone call.

* * *

Cherry twirled in front of the full-length mirror. 'Do you like it?' she asked Dino breathily.

'Pretty,' he replied, more concerned with how the evening would go, than Cherry's new dress.

'You don't like it.' She pouted.

'Honey, I do.' He caught her up in his arms and hugged her reassuringly. 'You look like a great big beautiful doll.'

152

'I'm your wife,' she announced proudly. 'Mrs Dino Foncetti!'

His stomach turned over with fear. In the entire thirty-one years he'd been alive he had never made one important decision without consulting his father. Now he had really done it. He had sneaked off that very afternoon and married Cherry before Joseph thought of some smart way of getting rid of her.

'Your father's going to like me,' Cherry said, as if reading his mind. 'You'll see, he really will. I can promise you that.'

'I know, I know,' Dino managed to say. 'But you gotta keep your pretty mouth closed about us being married. I'll tell him in my own way.'

'Tonight?'

'Yeah, sure, honey, tonight.'

She smiled. 'What a surprise it'll be! Me and your father meeting for the first time to talk about you and me getting married, and then boom – you'll tell him!'

'Yeah – boom.' Dino attempted to smile. It was a struggle.

* * *

Joseph Fonicetti arrived in the Magna Carter restaurant precisely at six forty-five. He inspected the dinner table and pronounced it suitable. The head waiter sighed with relief.

Working for Joseph Fonicetti a man learned to be meticulous.

'Bring me a glass of Perrier,' Joseph requested. 'And some of those little white cards.'

The waiter responded immediately, then stood at a respectful distance while Joseph scrawled on the placement cards in his atrocious handwriting.

At exactly two minutes to seven, David, his eldest son, arrived with his wife, Mia. They both embraced Joseph, and took their places at the table. They both ordered Perrier and sat quietly.

At exactly two minutes past seven Dino arrived with Cherry. He was holding her hand, but his palm was sweating so badly that her hand threatened to slip away.

'Cherry, meet my father, Joseph Fonicetti,' Dino said nervously.

Cherry stepped forward, wide-eyed. 'Mr Fonicetti, I have been so looking forward to this moment.'

Joseph beamed, 'So have I, my dear, so have I.' The girl was prettier than he'd expected. Dino had always gone for the sour-faced big-boobed kind before, this one was different. 'Sit right here, next to me. What'll you have to drink?'

Cherry's eyes didn't waver, but she had already noticed the Perrier bottles. 'Oh, Perrier water if I may – you don't mind, do you?'

'Mind? Of course not.' Smarter than he had expected.

Dino went to sit beside her.

Joseph waved him away. 'Down there, next to your sister-in-law.'

Dino moved obediently to the other end of the table and ordered a double scotch.

Susanna and Bernie arrived next. He did a double take when he saw Cherry. A part of the family? So soon?

Susanna rushed to kiss Joseph. 'Uncle Joe, you look younger every time I see you.' She blew kisses at David and Dino. They had been friends since childhood.

Then Carlos Brent made his entrance. A typical Carlos Brent entrance with noise and excitement and an entourage of six.

The dinner party was almost complete.

'Where's Nico Constantine?' asked Joseph. 'It's nearly a quarter after seven.'

Anyone who knew Joseph at all knew he was a stickler for punctuality.

Susanna looked at Bernie. 'Where *is* Nico?'

Bernie shrugged and tried to look suitably casual. 'He sent his apologies, hopes to make it later for coffee.'

'He's got a new girlfriend,' Susanna confided. 'I don't think she ever lets him out of bed. He's such a sex fiend.'

Joseph turned to Cherry. 'You're a friend of Nico's, aren't you?'

She smoothed down the front of her new pink dress. 'Nico's been like a father to me,' she said demurely.

I bet, thought Joseph. He was on to Cherry. Miss sweetness and light. She had dazzled Dino with the first clean pussy he'd seen in years.

He contemplated what it would take to get rid if her. Maybe Nico would know, after all he'd brought her into Dino's life, and he could take her right on out again.

She was amazingly pretty. Bad wife material. She'd be screwing around before the ink was dry on the marriage license.

Joseph glanced down the table at Mia. Now *she* was wife material.

'Mr Fonicetti,' Cherry gushed, 'you don't know how exciting this is for me. Meeting Dino, you . . .'

'Where are you from, dear?' Joseph asked. May as well find out her version of her background before he hired a private detective to dig out the truth.

* * *

As far as Bernie was concerned the dinner dragged on for ever. He needed it like he needed piles.

Susanna was playing girl wife again. Carlos was

throwing him fishy fake smiles. Mia and David were both as dull as each other. Dino was a nervous wreck. And Cherry – little Miss Blue Eyes – was all innocence and golden curls and not fooling crafty old Joseph Fonicetti one bit.

Bernie had been unable to contact Nico in London. No answer in his hotel room. So he'd left a message relaying the fact that everything was fine, so far. But how long would it be before it was noticed that Nico's handsome face was no longer in evidence? And how long could Bernie fool them with a mystery girlfriend who didn't even exist?

As if on cue, Joseph said, 'Hey, Bernie, where's Nico? I thought you said he'd be here for coffee.'

'I guess he got hung up.'

'I invite people for dinner, they usually come. I want to talk to Nico. It's business, have him come up to my suite later.'

Oh, sure. Just like that. Bernie was beginning to seriously consider the possibility of jetting back to L.A. the next day with Susanna. Get out while he was safe.

'If I see him,' he said lamely. 'Like he's taken off with this girl . . .'

'Taken off?' Joseph snapped. 'Dino, did you hear that?'

'What?' Dino jumped. His mind had been exploring the possibility of a honeymoon in Europe, far far away from his father.

'Nico Constantine has taken off,' Joseph said grimly.

'Not taken off,' Bernie said quickly, attempting a weak laugh. 'I mean he's around, but this girl, well, you know how it can be.'

'What girl?' Joseph enquired, his eyes suddenly steely.

'I don't know her name . . .'

'Does she work here?'

'I'm not sure.'

'So who is she? What does she do?'

Susanna joined in, 'Yes, who is this woman of mystery?'

Bernie could have belted her. He didn't like the look in Joseph's eyes. Joseph was one smart old man.

'I told you, I don't know. Some broad who's dragged him away from the tables all the way into her bed.'

'Everyone!' Cherry clapped her hands excitedly. 'I can't keep it to myself any longer! Today, this very afternoon, Dino and I got married!'

Bernie could have kissed her. It was one heck of a way to take everyone's mind off of Nico.

Chapter Fifteen

'What?' Nico could not believe what Hal was telling him.

'Fake,' Hal stated flatly. 'One helluva chunk of cut glass set in real platinum. A copy, a beaut, but the real thing it ain't.'

Nico suppressed an insane desire to laugh. 'I don't believe it!' he said.

'Start believing, kid. It's not worth more than a few hundred.'

Nico shook his head in amazement. So – Mrs Dean Costello had fooled him. Or had she? The old dear had never claimed that her ring was real. She had never handed him papers to prove its authenticity. She probably had the real thing locked up in a bank vault. Of course. It was obvious. A diamond that size – all the rich women had copies made of their gems. And excellent copies too. Good enough to fool everyone except the experts.

Nico was embarrassed. 'Hal, what can I say? I had no idea.'

Hal was friendly. 'I bet you didn't. Even I thought it was the real thing, and I have an eye – I can spot the real stuff a mile off. Listen, it was nice nearly doing business with you.' He prepared to leave. 'Give my best to Bernie. You leaving today?'

Nico shrugged. 'I have no idea what I'm going to do.'

'You know what you really need? A rich, old broad.' Hal laughed. 'Rich, old and grateful.' He warmed to his subject. 'Now I have a couple of hot ones flying in from Texas tomorrow. You want a million dollars – no problem. But you'll have to work for it . . .'

'How old?'

'Not spring chickens.'

'How old?'

'In their sixties, maybe creeping up to seventy . . . But you'd never know, what with silicone tits and face jobs and . . .'

'Forget it,' Nico interrupted.

'Suit yourself, only it's a winning game.'

Yeah. A winning game. That's what he really needed.

Hal left, and Nico paced his hotel room wondering what his next move should be. Alert Bernie. That had to be first. Tell him to get out of Vegas and stop covering for him.

Then what? How was he ever going to score half a million dollars?

How had he ever *lost* half a million dollars?

Gambling.

His bankroll was almost non-existent, but that didn't phase him. He picked up the phone and requested the manager.

Full Nico charm. 'Mr Graheme, I have a slight problem. My bank in Switzerland is transferring funds by tomorrow, no problem. In the meantime if you could let me have – say – five-hundred pounds in cash – and charge it to my bill I would be most grateful . . .'

* * *

The six dozen red roses arrived late afternoon. They were waiting for Fontaine when she returned to her house after the auditions. Mrs Walters had set them out in matching cut glass vases.

'Christ!' Fontaine exclaimed irritably. 'This place is beginning to look like a funeral parlour! I know I asked for fresh flowers, Mrs Walters, but this is ridiculous.'

Mrs Walters clucked her agreement, and handed her employer the card which had accompanied the roses.

Fontaine read it. The message was brief – just – 'Thank you. Nico.'

Thank you for what? For a great screw? For throwing him out? For what?

Fontaine tore the card into tiny pieces and let it flutter over the carpet.

Mrs Walters pursed her lips. Who would have to clear *that* up later? Her, of course.

'I don't want to be disturbed.' Fontaine sighed. 'I simply have to rest.'

'Your lawyer has phoned three times, Mrs Khaled, he says it's urgent that he arrange an appointment with you immediately.'

'How boring.'

'And Count Rispollo phoned.'

'Even more boring.'

'What shall I say if they call again, Mrs Khaled?'

'Tell them I am resting, and to phone back tomorrow.'

'Oh, and this arrived.' Mrs Walters produced a small package.

Fontaine took it from her and balanced it in her hand. Boucheron. Was it a token of Count Paulo's esteem?

'Wake me at eight o'clock.' She said, heading upstairs.

The thought occurred to her that maybe she should have brought Steve Valentine home with her. Personally seen to it that he had what it takes in all the right places.

Once that would have been exciting, only somehow the thrill of just another horny body was beginning to pall.

Now if it was Nico . . .

Screw Nico. She didn't want to think about him. Lousy hustler. Using her to smuggle his stuff through customs. Sharing her bed only to recover his ring.

She ripped open the packet from Boucheron, and read the card that fell out.

Same card. Same message. 'Thank you. Nico.'

Thoughtfully she stared at the diamond-encrusted heart. It was very lovely. She took it out of the box and held it in her hand.

Nico . . . He had been a very special lover . . .

* * *

So far so good. Nico was winning. Nothing sensational, but a beginning.

He had started the evening with a stake of a thousand pounds, and had managed to work up to twenty-five thousand. A promising beginning.

For a change everything seemed to be going his

way. And if his luck kept on track, who knew what could happen?

He was enjoying the ambience of a British gaming club. So different from the brashness of Vegas. There were busty female croupiers in low-cut dresses. Discreet pit bosses. Sexy girls serving drinks.

The atmosphere was that of a rather elegant club.

Nico lit up a long thin cigar, and moved from a blackjack table to roulette. The limit was not as high as he would have wished, and he was unable to bet more than five-hundred on black. It came up. Good. But certainly not good enough. He needed to get into a high-stake poker game, and he looked around for someone who might be able to arrange it.

The manager seemed a likely prospect, and sure enough he was. He recommended another club which would be happy to accommodate Nico with poker, backgammon or whatever he wished.

Nico took a taxi there.

He had tried to telephone Bernie earlier, but had been unable to reach him. Now he decided to concentrate on making one big score.

* * *

'Hmmm . . .' Fontaine stood in the doorway and surveyed the action at Hobo. 'Well, I suppose I shouldn't expect miracles. It is his first night.'

Polly nodded. 'He looks good though, don't you think?'

Fontaine watched Steve through narrowed kaleidoscope eyes. 'He doesn't have the walk,' she observed.

'What walk?' Polly asked.

'The John Travolta cock thrust. You know what I mean.'

Polly couldn't help giggling. Cock thrust. It sounded like something you did in an aeroplane!

Steve strolled toward them, clad in a cheap black pinstripe suit, shirt and tie.

'Mrs Khaled. A table for how many?'

'Your look is wrong, Steve,' she snapped. 'You're running a club, not your uncle's wedding.'

'Sorry.'

'Don't worry, obviously they're a touch more formal in Ealing. Now, let me see,' she said, reaching for his tie, untying and removing it. Then she unbuttoned his shirt three buttons. 'That's better. Tomorrow I'll take you shopping.'

Oh God! Shades of Tony! How well she remembered their first meeting. A disaster. He had possessed an animal charm, a sexy walk, but that was about all. And in bed – nothing but raw ability. She had seen his potential, and trained him to make full use of it in every way. Tony had been a swift learner, and then he'd gotten too big for his newly acquired Gucci loafers.

Now Steve stood before her. Raw material. Was it worth building him into a monster too?

Count Paulo, who was lucky enough to be escorting Polly and Fontaine, gave Steve a dirty look. 'Mrs Khaled's table?'

'Of course,' Steve jumped to attention.

Count Paulo ordered the obligatory champagne, and asked Fontaine to dance.

'You dance with him, Polly,' Fontaine commanded. 'At least try and make the place look busy.'

* * *

Nico's run of luck continued to the tune of fifty thousand pounds. He was smart enough to quit as soon as the cards began to turn.

He felt elated, so elated that he risked a phone call to Fontaine.

A disgruntled housekeeper, obviously woken from a deep sleep, informed him that madam was out.

Then he spotted a very tall blonde in a very revealing dress. He'd noticed her earlier in the evening at the other gaming club. She was certainly striking. Not a fresh-faced beauty, nor a sophisticated Fontaine. But very, very striking.

She smiled at him across the room, and he smiled back.

He thought no more about her.

He collected his coat from reception, tipped the man at the desk handsomely, and signalled the door-man for a cab.

She appeared just as he was climbing in. 'Can you give me a lift?' Her voice was soothingly husky. 'I am escaping from an over-amorous Arab, and if I don't vanish immediately I'm in trouble.'

Nico raised a quizzical eyebrow. 'You are?'

'Please?'

'Hop in. I always help beautiful women in trouble.'

She smiled. 'I knew you'd say that.'

'You did?'

'You look like Omar Sharif – so why shouldn't you sound like him?'

'I'm not an Arab, I'm Greek.'

'I know that. There's no way I would've shared a taxi with an Arab, thank you.'

'How did you know I was Greek?'

She opened her purse, took out a compact, and inspected her face. 'I didn't know what you were, I just knew you weren't an Arab.' She clicked the compact shut. 'Hi – I'm Lynn.' Formally she extended her hand. 'And you?'

'Nico Constantine.'

'Greek name, but you sound American.'

'Yes, I've lived in L.A. for the last ten years. Now, where can I drop you?'

Lynn mock pouted. 'Trying to get rid of me so soon?'

Nico laughed. 'Not at all.'

'Did I hear you tell the cab driver the Dorchester?'

'That's where I'm staying.'

'They make the best scrambled eggs in town, and I'm starving.'

'Scrambled eggs, huh?'

'If you've never had them, you must try.'

The restaurant will be closed.'

'And room service will be open.'

*   *   *

Vanessa, Leonard, and a large group of people arrived at Hobo as Fontaine's guests.

She watched the women's reactions to Steve. Nothing special.

'Do you fancy him?' she whispered to Vanessa.

'He's not Tony,' Vanessa replied.

'Fuck Tony,' Fontaine said crisply. 'I'm sick to death of hearing about Tony. He's not the only stud in the world!' She drained her champagne glass, and gestured for more.

'He is quite cute,' Vanessa ventured.

'Cute! Christ! Cute is hardly what I'm looking for.'

The evening sped by in a haze of champagne.

168

Fontaine allowed herself to get delightfully, pleasantly bombed.

Count Paulo clutched her in his arms on the dance floor and declared undying love and lust. 'We must be in bed together soon,' he panted, 'my whole body screams for you.'

He rubbed embarrassingly against her, and she wished he'd take his juvenile Italian horniness back to Italy with him.

She danced with Leonard.

'How about a cosy lunch one day, just the two of us?' Leonard suggested.

God save her from middle-aged husbands who considered her fair game.

Goodbyes were said in the early hours of the morning on the sidewalk outside Hobo. Ricky stood obediently holding the door of the Rolls open while Fontaine, Polly, and Count Paulo piled in.

'Drop Miss Brand first,' Fontaine ordered. 'Then Count Rispollo.'

'Yes, Mrs Khaled.'

Polly managed a surreptitious wink as she was dropped off. 'Later?' she whispered.

'You bet,' Ricky replied, *sotto voce*.

Count Paulo was complaining loudly about being dropped at his hotel. 'Tonight I thought we would be together,' he said bitterly. 'I come all this way to see you, and you treat me like . . . like dirt.'

'I'm tired,' Fontaine replied coolly. 'Maybe tomorrow. Call me.'

A disappointed Count Paulo was deposited at his hotel.

'Home, Ricky,' instructed Fontaine.

Ricky glanced at the clock. Four o'clock in the bleedin' morning. He hoped she wasn't expecting him bright and early at ten a.m. By the time he made it back to Polly's and gave her a good seeing to, well, he'd need some sleep, wouldn't he?

They arrived at Fontaine's Pelham Crescent house. Ricky jumped out of the Rolls and held the door open for her.

She yawned openly and sighed. Dawn was beginning to break. Her kaleidoscope eyes swept over him. 'Coming in for an early morning cup of tea, Ricky?'

* * *

Nico and Lynn made love in his hotel suite. A room-service trolley bearing two plates of congealed scrambled eggs stood forlornly in the centre of the living room. Lynn was accomplished, striking, pleasant. The sex was enjoyable. Nico wished he hadn't been tempted. She was just another female. A beautiful body – yes, but a stranger. And somehow sex with strangers was not the way he wanted to lead his life anymore. He was too old for one-night stands. And too smart. And he wished he was with Fontaine beneath her black silk sheets exchanging bodily fluids.

'That was memorable,' Lynn said, getting up from the bed.

Nico nodded his agreement, hoping she would dress and leave.

She stretched, naked and cat-like. 'Are you into bondage?'

'What?'

'Bondage. You know, being tied up and beaten. The Arabs love it.'

'I told you, I'm not an Arab.'

'I know.' She arched her back, then touched her toes. Her body was somewhat sinewy. 'You're a Greek who talks American.' She picked up her dress from the floor and started to pull it on. 'And you're also a dumb son-of-a-bitch who had better pay back the money you owe the Fonicettis or you're going to find yourself an unrecognizable son-of-a-bitch. Am I making myself clear?'

'What did you say?' Nico sat up in bed, shocked.

Lynn fiddled with the zipper on her dress. Her smoky voice was very sensuous. 'You heard me. I'm a messenger, so you had better listen very, very carefully.' She searched for her spike-heeled shoes and put them on. 'You have a week, seven days, no credit.

171

Understand?' She picked up her purse and moved towards the door. She paused and smiled. 'Every cent, Nico, or . . . well . . . they're going to cut your balls off, and wouldn't that be a shame?'

She exited, closing the door quietly behind her.

* * *

'Isn't this fun?' Fontaine watched Ricky through slitted eyes as he poured the tea.

He wasn't sure whether to answer or not. The truth was he didn't know how to act at all.

'You know,' Fontaine murmured thoughtfully, 'you're really rather sexy. Why didn't I think of using *you* for the club?'

'Sugar, Mrs Khaled?'

'No, thank you.' She turned her back on him. 'Bring the tea up to the bedroom, Ricky, yours as well.'

He stood in the kitchen and watched her go. Then quick as a flash he whipped out a tray and put the two cups of tea on it. 'Ricky m'boy,' he muttered to himself, 'I think you just got lucky.'

'Ricky,' her slightly drunken voice called from the top of the stairs, 'are you coming?'

I will be in a minute, he thought. Polly would just have to wait.

Chapter Sixteen

Bernie, Susanna and Cherry sat in silence aboard Carlos Brent's private plane, each of them in deep thought.

Susanna smiled slightly. The shit had hit – Bernie's charming expression, fortunately it hadn't flown in her direction.

Cherry sobbed quietly, occasionally dabbing at her baby-blue eyes with a silk monogrammed handkerchief taken from one of Dino's drawers.

Bernie sat stoically. Mr Fall Guy. Mr Schmuck. It was just good luck he was connected to Carlos Brent, even if it was only a fragile connection. If he hadn't been. If Susanna had not intervened on his behalf. Well, he didn't like to think what would have happened.

Bernie reflected on the previous evening. It all seemed like a bad fucking dream. First, it was pure shit-luck that Joseph Fonicetti had decided to throw a dinner party. Second, the fact that Nico was an invited guest. And third, that Cherry and Dino had sneaked off and gotten married.

What a joke that was. What a disaster.

Joseph Fonicetti was far too canny an old animal to let anything slide past him. And the fact that Nico owed – and owed big – was reason enough for him to be suspicious when Nico failed to show. When Cherry announced that she and Dino were married, the party had really taken off.

Joseph Fonicetti did not like surprises, especially of that kind. He'd risen from the table, small mean eyes burning in his nut brown face. 'Is this fuckin' true?' he'd screamed at Dino. 'You gonna tell me you married the dumb cunt?'

Cherry had joined in then, blue eyes tearful but determined. 'How dare you call me that,' she'd said, looking at Dino for support.

Dino had slunk down in his chair. How could he argue with his father? The unfortunate truth was that she *was* a dumb cunt for opening up her mouth.

'Get me Nico Constantine, cut out the bullshit and find him,' Joseph demanded.

Bernie had visibly blanched, he did not know what to say.

Joseph sensed this immediately. 'He's still here, right, Bernie?' His voice was menacing.

Susanna cut in quickly with, 'Of course he is, Uncle Joe.'

Joseph ignored her. 'Check it out, David. I want that son-of-a-bitch, Nico, and I want him now.' He indicated a by now sobbing Cherry. 'She's his – this fuckin' Barbie doll. He can take her out of our lives.'

'Mr Fonicetti!' Cherry had gulped. 'I told you, Dino and I are married.'

'Find out where the stupid fuck did it, and take care of that too, David,' Joseph snapped. 'And get me Nico, pronto. There's also the matter of the money he owes us. Dino was supposed to take care of that, but he's been too busy taking care of his cock.' At this point Joseph had burst into a stream of angry Italian, a language that had stayed with him since childhood.

Carlos Brent had risen from the table, gone to Joseph, and put his arm around him.

The dinner party was over.

So was Cherry and Dino's marriage.

So was Nico when they found out he had split.

And so was Bernie when they found out he had aided and abetted.

Quickly he'd put his arm around Susanna. 'Let's get married again,' he'd suggested. 'We've had such a great time this last couple of days.'

'Anything to save your ass, huh, Bernie?' But she'd grinned when she'd said it.

Naturally it had not taken them long to find out that Nico was gone.

Bernie had been hauled up to the Fonicetti penthouse for questioning. Susanna had insisted on accompanying him. To save his own ass he'd been forced to tell them where Nico was.

'We'll take care of it,' Joseph had muttered ominously.

'He only went so he could raise the money to pay you,' Bernie had insisted. 'He's probably on his way back now.'

'Sure, sure.' Joseph stared him down with his mean little eyes. 'Remember one thing in life, Bernie. Loyalty. But don't fuck it up. Loyalty to the right people. When you knew Nico couldn't pay you should have come to me immediately. No hesitation. You understand?'

Bernie had nodded vigorously.

'But you're young, you have a lot to learn. And I myself have loyalty to Carlos Brent. So you are lucky. You understand?'

'He understands, Uncle Joe,' Susanna had said, kissing the old man on the cheek. 'It won't happen again. And thank you.'

So Bernie's balls were intact. Only now they belonged to Susanna again.

* * *

Cherry shared an apartment in Hollywood with two other girls. They were both away. One on a fishing trip with a porno-movie star. The other on location in Oregon.

Cherry wandered around the empty apartment in a daze. It had all happened so quickly. One moment she was Mrs Dino Fonicetti. The next just plain Cherry, unsuccessful actress.

It wasn't fair. What was wrong with her? What made her unsuitable material to be Dino's wife? Why did his father automatically hate her?

She stared at her exquisite reflection in the mirror. Blonde hair. Blue eyes. Perfect features. With Dino's dark good looks, what beautiful babies they would have made together.

Dino. His behaviour had not been very nice. Allowing his father to call her horrible names.

She gave a long drawn-out sigh, walked in the tiny bathroom, removed a line of drying underclothes from across the bath, selected her favourite bubbles, and started to run the water.

Then she stripped off her clothes and stepped into the bath.

* * *

* * *

'Operator, try that number again please.' Bernie bounced his daughter Starr on his knee, and tried to locate Nico for the fifth time.

Susanna was busy unpacking his clothes. On the way from the airport she'd insisted on picking up all his things from Nico's rented house.

'We can do it tomorrow,' Bernie had complained.

'I want to feel you're really back,' Susanna had insisted. 'Not just sharing my bed for a night.'

As she unpacked she moaned constantly, 'Look at these shirts! My God what kind of a laundry did you send these to! Bernie, these socks should have been thrown away, they're full of holes. Oh no! This is my favourite sweater on you, and you've got a cigarette burn in it. How could you?'

Bernie tuned out, and concentrated on reaching Nico. The least he could do was warn him.

'I think we should have a small wedding, nothing flashy, something tasteful, with Starr as a bridesmaid. What do you think, Bernie?' Susanna enquired.

'Good idea,' Bernie said, not really listening.

'Daddy suggested his house in Palm Springs. We could fly everyone up. That would be fun, wouldn't it?'

'Sure.' Goddamn Daddy again. Same old, same old.

'I'll wear blue – and how about you in a blue suit so that we match? And Starr in blue frills. Oh Bernie, it's all so exciting!'

There was nothing Susanna liked better than planning a party, or a wedding for that matter. Bernie remembered, with a feeling of dread, their famous Saturday night intimate dinner parties for fifty or sixty. Shit. This time he would have to put his foot down.

'We're ringing Mr Constantine's suite,' the hotel operator's voice said.

Three rings and Nico answered.

'I've been trying to reach you for days,' Bernie exclaimed. 'The shit has—'

Chapter Seventeen

'Hit. I know.' Nico replied.

'How do you know? What's happened?' Bernie stuttered.

'They have given me a very generous seven days to come up with the money.'

'And the ring?'

'Fake, my friend.'

'What'll you do?'

'I'll think of something.'

'Listen, Nico. It wasn't my fault they found out. I tried. I kept it going for days. What happened is a long story.'

'Save it. I'll be back to hear it personally. In one piece, I hope.'

'I'm glad you can take it so calmly.'

'What other way is there?'

'If you need me I'm at Susanna's.'

'Reconciliation?'

'I'll explain.'

'Keep hold of your balls. Don't let her twist them too hard.'

Nico hung up the phone. He was calm. His energies could not be wasted on panicking. He'd sat and thought from the moment of Lynn's departure.

There were three moves that he could make. One, he could take his fifty thousand pounds winnings and escape to South America. Two, he could change his name and start a new life. Three, he could pay them the money he owed.

Three was the only answer. But how could he get the money?

He fell asleep still trying to work it out.

* * *

Fontaine awoke to the smell and a taste of a hangover, and a loud hammering on her locked bedroom door. She felt positively dreadful.

'Mrs Khaled,' a voice assaulted her, 'it's past twelve, I have your breakfast tray.'

'Leave it outside, Mrs Walters,' she groaned.

Her headache was lethal. She tried to remember

fragments of the previous evening, and suddenly she did.

Oh God! Ricky. He was still asleep in her bed. She sat up and surveyed her bedroom. It looked like a party had taken place.

And it had. A party for two. Talk about shades of Lady Chatterley's lover!

Sliding from her bed, she put on a silk kimono, and thought about how she could get rid of him. Mrs Walters wouldn't be shocked that she'd had a man spend the night, she was used to it. But the fact that it was her chauffeur! No! It was all too much.

'Ricky.' She gave him a short sharp shove. 'Get up and get the hell out!'

'What?' Blearily he opened his eyes. 'Where am I?' Then he remembered. 'Oh yeah, course. C'm here, darlin', I'll give you a bit more of what you enjoyed last night.'

She withered him with a look. 'Forget about last night, Ricky. And I am not darling, I am Mrs Khaled, and don't you forget it. Now kindly dress and go.'

He sat up in bed. 'You giving me the old elbow?'

'If you mean am I firing you, the answer is no, as long as you remember that last night was a figment of your imagination.'

Bloody hell! Some figment. He had a very good recollection of Mrs Khaled sitting astride him in nothing but a mink coat and his chauffeur's cap yelling, 'First one to the gate is the winner!' Bloody hell!

Fontaine retired into the bathroom, and Ricky dressed quickly. He let himself out of the locked bedroom, nearly tripped over the breakfast tray, and sneaked downstairs.

Mrs Walters was busy dusting. She threw him a look of disdain accompanied by a disgusted sniff.

'Morning, Mrs Walters,' he said cheerfully.

She turned her back on him.

* * *

Backgammon had always been a game Nico had excelled at. He presented himself at a London club and exercised his skills. London had no lack of back-gammon hustlers, but Nico was more than a match for them. He spent the afternoon at play, and emerged in the early evening several thousand pounds richer.

Not bad, but hardly enough to help.

He needed advice. He called Hal.

They met in Trader Vic's for a drink, Hal resplend-ent in a new white suit.

Nico fingered Hal's lapel. 'Nice material,' he remarked.

'Gotta look the best for my ladies,' Hal said. 'They're here. If I play it right I could own half of

Detroit by tomorrow morning! Sure you won't join us for dinner?'

'Only if they have five-hundred-thousand dollars to hand my way,' Nico said wryly.

Hal laughed. 'Five years solid fucking could probably get you that.'

Nico grimaced. 'I need it a little sooner.' His black eyes fixed on Hal, almost hypnotic in their intensity. 'I am deadly serious about needing the money. I blew out of Vegas owing, thought the ring would cover it. Now,' he gestured hopelessly, 'they've found me. They sent a woman messenger. I thought she was a beautiful girl looking to get laid. She got laid all right, then she delivered the message. Seven days. They mean business. You know it and I know it. Any suggestions?'

Hal summoned the pretty Asian waitress and ordered another navy grog. He was sympathetic. But not that sympathetic. He liked Nico, but if trouble was coming his way, Hal wanted to be long gone.

'Let me get some details here,' Hal said, stalling for time while he thought of a fast excuse to be on his way. 'Who do you owe? And how much?'

'I wasn't kidding you,' Nico said glumly. 'I owe the Fonicettis five-hundred-and-fifty grand.'

Hal let out a long low whistle. 'Jeez! I know old Joe Fonicetti. Are you gonna tell me they let you run up markers for that much? It's impossible.'

'Not when you lose six-hundred-thou of your own money up front,' Nico explained.

Hal whistled again. 'You're in trouble, my friend. Big, big trouble.'

The Asian waitress delivered his drink, and smiled inscrutably at both of them.

'I've never fucked an Asian girl,' Hal said absently as she walked away. 'So tell me, Nico. Who was your lady messenger? Did they send a girl from Vegas?'

Nico shook his head. 'She was English. Told me her name was Lynn.'

'Tall? Hot body?'

Nico nodded. 'You know her?'

'She used to be a dancer on TV. Never made it until she met the man himself.'

'What man would that be?'

'Feathers. Lynn's his right-hand woman. She's one tough lady – into judo, the martial arts. You were lucky you only got fucked!'

'Thanks a lot.'

'Maybe I could talk to Feathers,' Hal said. 'Try to figure something out.'

'You'd do that?' Nico said.

'Problem is – we're not on the best of terms right now. A debt. It's dragged on.'

'How much?'

'Five-thousand. I keep him happy with a payment

here, a payment there. But he'd be a lot happier to see a lump sum.'

'Pay him. I got it. Call it a fee for your help.'

'You don't have to do that,' Hal said.

'I know, but if you can work out a deal with Feathers, then maybe *he* can work out something with Fonicetti. Perhaps an instalment plan like you had. What do you think?'

Hal nodded slowly. 'Whatever I can do. It's worth a shot.'

Nico patted him on the shoulder. 'Thanks. I appreciate it.'

* * *

Wild-looking models in exotic underclothes undulated slinkily down the catwalk.

Fontaine, sitting at a ringside table, openly yawned.

'Aren't you enjoying it?' Vanessa asked anxiously. The fashion show was raising money for one of her charities and she desperately wanted it to be a success.

'I never did get turned on gaping at other women's bodies,' Fontaine replied. 'Aren't there any male models? You know – horny little nineteen-year-olds in nothing but their jockeys and a smile?'

'Oh, Fontaine! Really! It's the clothes you're supposed to be looking at.'

'Hmmm . . .' Fontaine allowed her gaze to wander around the restaurant where the fashion show was taking place. Tables and tables of boring women, all dressed in the latest most expensive clothes. Just as she was.

Was this what her life was all about? Fashion and getting fucked. Both were beginning to pall.

'I have to leave soon,' she whispered to Vanessa. 'Got to meet with my lawyer. The boring old fart is threatening me with the workhouse if I don't come up with some money soon. The pittance Benjamin pays me hardly covers my weekly expenses. I simply have to get Hobo back in action.'

'You will,' Vanessa replied. 'When you put your mind to it, nothing can stop you.'

'I know, I always get what I want. But surely you can see, Vanessa, that's just an illusion I create.'

Vanessa looked at her friend disbelievingly. She envied Fontaine, and could never imagine her being dissatisfied. All the women envied Fontaine's lifestyle – even if they pretended not to. She had beauty, freedom and certainly no visible lack of money.

Vanessa had a rich husband, four children, an overweight body, and not a moment to call her own. Fontaine had a seemingly never-ending supply of fanciable young men. Vanessa had only managed two affairs in twelve long years of marriage.

'I'm so bored!' Fontaine stated. 'Shall I tell you a

secret, Vanessa? Just between you and me. Don't you dare tell anyone.'

Vanessa nodded, her eyes shining. 'Tell me! Tell me!' she pleaded.

'Last night, I was so bored that I screwed my chauffeur.'

'You didn't!' Vanessa exclaimed, suitably shocked.

'I certainly did. And let me tell you it was even more boring than being bored!'

Vanessa frowned. 'Wasn't he any good?'

'All the attributes, my darling. Big cock, firm balls and lovely thighs. But BORING!'

Vanessa blinked. Fontaine was the most outrageous and outspoken person she had ever met.

'The thing is,' Fontaine continued, 'when I was married to Benjamin, all these little adventures seemed so much more exciting. Now, well, it's all so bloody predictable.'

'I've met someone—' Vanessa began.

Fontaine ignored her, and continued speaking. 'Now that man on the plane – Nico. Not my usual scene at all, darling. But I must say, with him, it was just . . . different. He was so – I don't know, it seems a silly word for me to use, but he was so worldly and amusing. Maybe I made a mistake throwing him out.'

'I never did get to meet him—' Vanessa started to say.

They were interrupted by the arrival of Sammy at their table.

'Mornin', gels! Havin' a wonderful time?' he said, sitting down.

'Do have a seat,' Fontaine murmured.

'Ah, her highness is on form today.' Sammy said, pouring himself some wine. 'Listen, darlin's, I want you to take a look at my new collection.' He indicated the models, now in sports clothes. 'Anything you want – it's yours.'

'You're in a very generous mood today,' Fontaine said. 'How come?'

''Cause you're gorgeous, darlin'. Bit old for me, but—'

'Piss off, Sammy,' Fontaine said mildly.

'No offence, my darlin'. I like 'em nineteen. Everyone to their own. Know what I mean?'

Fontaine couldn't help smiling. Sammy was a genuine character, and a likeable one.

'Your clothes aren't my usual style,' she said.

'So wear 'em at the beach. Big deal. Pick out what you want, it'll be good for me if you're seen wearin' 'em.'

Fontaine ticked off a halter sun-dress on her programme, and a white track suit. Actually his designs were quite fun.

'Ready for me to take over Hobo yet?' Sammy asked with a cheeky grin.

'I'll tell you what, Sammy, I'm starting to give it serious thought.'

He chuckled. 'Really?'

'Why not? You *are* Mr Personality.'

'Oh, yeah, that I am,' he boasted.

'I think you could be quite an attraction. Not in the same way as Tony of course.'

'Of course.'

'But in your own way . . .'

'Hang on. I was only joking y' know. I've got a business to run.'

Fontaine fixed him with her kaleidoscope eyes. 'Sammy?' she said briskly, 'how does the idea of becoming a partner in Hobo appeal to you?'

Chapter Eighteen

Bernie settled back into married life like a mouse into a trap.

Susanna gaily made second wedding plans, nagged him continually about this and that, and phoned dear old Daddy Carlos for a loving conversation at least twice a day.

'Find out what they're doing about Nico,' Bernie instructed.

'How can I?' Susanna replied, all girlish innocence.

'Don't give me that shit,' Bernie snapped. 'You know and I know and so does all of Hollywood that Carlos Brent has connections that make Washington look like a kiddies' tea party. He probably owns the fucking Forum hotel for all we know.'

'Don't be ridiculous. Daddy's so called "connections" are all in your head.'

'Bullfuckingshit. I want you to find Nico. He's a good friend of mine, and I don't want anything happening to him.'

Susanna sniped, 'He didn't seem to care so much about what happened to you, did he? Left you holding the can, and if you and I hadn't gotten back together, well, you know how Daddy feels about your treatment of me.'

'Yeah, sure. He'd have been only too pleased to have me pushing up cacti in the fucking desert.'

Susanna made a face. 'You're such a smartass, you really are. What a stupid thing to say.'

Two hours later she casually relayed the information that Nico had been allowed a week to pay.

'You see,' she said. 'Uncle Joseph is a kind and generous man.'

'Uncle Joseph! Only *you* would call one of the biggest mobsters in Vegas, uncle.'

Susanna pursed her lips. 'The trouble with you, Bernie, is that you think everyone even remotely associated with Vegas is a gangster. Uncle Joseph is a perfectly respectable hotel owner.'

'Yeah, and the Pope's Jewish!'

Bernie waited until Susanna and Starr went out to order their wedding outfits, then he hurried up to the bedroom, and checked out Susanna's clothes closet to see if her safe was still there. It was, concealed behind a wall of shoes. It occurred to him that she might have had the combination changed, but as he tried it he realized it was the same.

The safe door swung open, and facing him was her myriad collection of jewellery boxes, each one containing a diamond-encrusted gift from her father. Also in the safe were the one-hundred-thousand dollars in cash that Carlos had handed them as a wedding present. One-hundred neat, crisp, thousand-dollar bills. Untouched. Intact. And half his, although Susanna had never allowed him anywhere near it.

What kind of a dumb idiot hung onto cash when the money could have been sitting in a bank accumulating interest? His ex-soon-to-be-present-wife – dear Susanna.

'We'll keep it as emergency money,' she'd stated five years ago. And that was the last he'd seen of it.

Susanna didn't realize that he knew the safe's combination, but he'd watched her fetch a necklace from it one night, and the numerals had stuck.

Hey – half was his. He was entitled.

He extracted fifty one-thousand-dollar bills, and replaced them with singles at the bottom of the stack.

If he could help Nico with the money – then that's exactly what he planned to do.

Chapter Nineteen

Sammy said yes, just like that.

He surprised everyone, including himself. But what was money for if not to spend it? And he had always had a hankering to front a club. It was the extrovert in him.

'I'm not another stud tryin' to creep into your bed,' he warned Fontaine.

'God forbid!' she exclaimed.

So they set a deal, shook hands, and then they were in business together.

For Fontaine it was a lifesaver. Her finances really were in a dire state. She needed Hobo to be a success again.

Once involved, Sammy did not hang about. He hired nineteen-year-old twin disc jockeys – a girl and a boy. New waiters, all young, ambitious and highly paid. He liked Steve Valentine, and decided to keep him on as a backup. He sent him for a decent haircut and to a stylist for a makeover. The difference was startling.

'It's amazing, you've given him style,' Fontaine said.

'Course I have,' agreed Sammy. 'Now let's concentrate on changing the menu, and getting this place going again.'

Fontaine and Sammy were an odd couple. Working together until all hours. Planning, laughing, joking. To their mutual surprise they actually liked each other. Nothing sexual – purely platonic. Sammy was amazed at Fontaine's sense of humour. When she wasn't busy acting out her bullshit sexy Mrs Khaled number, she was witty, down to earth and a lot of fun to be with.

Fontaine found that she adored Sammy. He was warm and humorous and natural.

She was so busy that she even forgot about sex. At night she was happy to collapse into her bed alone after a hard day at the club.

Sammy had decided they should close Hobo down for a few days while they made their changes, then reopen with a huge party. 'Expensive, but worth it my darlin',' he'd assured her.

She agreed. She didn't want to tell him that her

lawyer was now suggesting that she should sell her house and car to meet her mounting debts. Her lawyer was an asshole. She would prove to him how wrong he was.

She forgot about her problems and launched into planning a lavish party. Champagne and caviar for two-hundred of London's most interesting and fun people. What did a few more bills matter? In for a penny, in for the whole bloody lot.

* * *

It took Hal almost a week to arrange a meeting between Nico and Feathers.

'He's not an easy man to get to see,' Hal explained. 'And a meet with one of his minions would do you no good at all. But don't worry, I've explained your situation, and he'll see you tonight.'

'Christ!' Nico exclaimed. 'Tomorrow my seven days are up. This is cutting it too fine for my nerves.'

'Feathers has connections in all the right places. I'm sure he can work it out. Don't forget, he's in direct contact with the Fonicettis, your debt is his concern now.'

Nico had spent an uneasy few days. His luck at the gaming tables had held, and his original stake was up to ninety-thousand pounds. He planned to hand the money to Feathers as a sign of good intent. But how was he going to come up with the rest?

The thought of getting out of town occurred to him daily. But to return to Los Angeles seemed even more dangerous; he felt safer where he was.

He'd telephoned Fontaine on three occasions and, even though he'd left messages, she never returned his calls. Not so much as a note to thank him for the diamond heart or the six dozen roses. Perhaps she was the bitch everyone said she was.

He'd put her out of his mind, and concentrated on the tables.

Hal picked him up outside the Dorchester at eight thirty precisely.

'Nine o'clock meeting. We can't be late or early. Feathers is funny like that, so we'll play it safe and ride around the block when we get there.'

'Where does he live?' Nico asked.

'He never sees anyone at his home,' Hal explained. 'One of his casinos is where we're meeting.'

* * *

Fontaine surveyed herself in the full-length mirror one final time before leaving.

How could you beat perfection?

The long tube of black silk jersey, the blood-red embroidered Chinese kimono, the Madam Butterfly hairdo. Startling, but very effective. If she was in America now her photo would certainly appear on the front page of *Women's Wear Daily.*

She swept downstairs. Mrs Walters was duly impressed. 'Oh, you do look lovely, Mrs Khaled.'

Fontaine accepted the compliment as her due, and nodded regally. 'Is Ricky outside?' she asked.

'Yes, madam, and the count is waiting in the living room.'

Oh God! The count. She'd forgotten about him. But then it certainly wouldn't have looked right if she had arrived at her own party without an escort.

Count Paulo waited impatiently. He leapt up when Fontaine entered the room.

'*Bellissimo! Bellissimo!*' he exclaimed, kissing her hand.

'Calm down, sweetheart,' Fontaine drawled. 'Don't get yourself all excited.'

Who would have thought that she'd ever be bored by a twenty-five-year-old horny Italian count? But she was. Indeed she was.

* * *

Lynn met them at the reception desk. She acted like she had never set eyes on Nico before.

'Please follow me, gentlemen,' she said formally, 'Mr Feathers is expecting you.'

She led them through a door marked 'Private' which in turn led them down a long narrow corridor.

'Great ass,' Hal managed to mutter as they followed Lynn.

She stopped at another door marked 'Private' and knocked three times.

A male voice called for them to come in.

They entered a luxurious office. Feathers sat behind an ornate desk. He was a big man with a taste for flashy suits and collared shirts. His face was night-club white and pasty, and his greased-down hair was very obviously dyed black. In spite of the cheapness of his look he managed to throw out an aura of sinis-ter and powerful menace.

He studied Nico through surprisingly small bloodshot eyes. Then he extended an even more surprisingly beautifully manicured hand, gave a dead fish kind of handshake and said, 'Take a seat, Nico. Hal, why don't you let Lynn take you for a walk.'

Hal nodded. 'Sure, sure,' he said.

Lynn directed a cold smile Hal's way. 'Come along, fat ass.' Her voice was as sensuous as ever. 'The big boys want to talk.'

She led Hal out of the room.

'Drink?' Feathers barked.

'Vodka,' Nico said.

Feathers snapped his fingers, and a previously unnoticed hood stepped from the background and opened up a rather garish 1940s cocktail cabinet.

'Vodka,' snapped Feathers, 'and order me up a weak tea and some biscuits.'

The hood nodded obligingly. He looked like he belonged in a 1940s gangster movie.

'So,' Feathers said. 'You're Nico Constantine. I am interested meeting a man who can play such a dangerous game with his life.'

Nico shrugged. 'I always intended to pay the Fonicettis back.'

'That's what they all say. Some of them even say it when their balls are decorating their ears, and their kneecaps are hanging by a thread.'

'You don't have to threaten me. I came here to try and work things out.'

'Good, Nico. Good. Glad to hear it.' Feathers leaned back in his chair. 'I understand your luck at the tables has been remarkable since you've been in London.'

'Not that remarkable, but I can make a substantial deposit toward my debt.' Nico said, accepting a giant tumbler of neat vodka from the hood.

'Excellent. Of course, while you're in London your debt with the Fonicettis is my concern. We have a mutual agreement.'

Nico nodded. 'I understand that.'

'The Fonicettis were not thrilled by your sudden secretive departure. If only you had discussed things with them . . .'

Nico could feel himself getting irritated. He didn't like Feathers. He didn't like being lectured.

'Can you help me postpone the rest of the debt?' he asked abruptly.

'I can get you an extension,' Feathers said blandly. 'If you co-operate on a minor hustle.'

'What sort of hustle?' Nico asked, already suspicious.

'Nothing illegal, just slightly bent.' Feathers laughed, a particularly nasty laugh. 'Do you really feel you have a choice?' he asked.

'There's always a choice in life.' Nico replied shortly.

Feathers' small mean eyes darkened. 'Not for you. Not if you want to remain in good health.'

His tea arrived on a tray, accompanied by a selection of sweet biscuits.

Nico gulped a slug of vodka. He had an insane desire to get out of there. 'What's the hustle?' he asked again.

'A certain horse is running in a big race next Saturday. This horse is the favourite, an out and out winner. We want the horse to lose. We want you to arrange it.'

Nico frowned. 'How can I do that?'

'The horse is called Garbo. It belongs to Vanessa and Leonard Grant. The jockey, Sandy Roots, is giving a regular screwing to Mrs Grant, and while her husband might not mind, Sandy's wife would be more than put out. She's a lovely girl, daughter of top trainer, Charley Watson.' Feathers paused to dunk a biscuit in his tea. 'Now, if Charley got a whiff of what was going on, then Sandy may as well pack up and leave the business.'

'I don't understand,' Nico said puzzled. 'What does this all have to do with me?'

'Easy. Vanessa and Leonard Grant. Best friends of Fontaine Khaled.'

'So?'

'So we know all about you and Mrs Khaled. The plane. The night together.'

'We're no longer in touch,' Nico said quickly.

Feathers coughed. 'You'd better arrange to be. The Grants are having a house party this weekend. Mrs Khaled is already invited. So are the Roots and Charley Watson. It'll be easy for you to get an invite, you'll fit right in with that lot.'

Nico hesitated. 'I don't know,' he said uncertainly. There was no way he wanted to use Fontaine again. Once was enough.

Feathers' tone was sharp. 'You join the weekend party, you persuade Sandy Roots to throw the race, and if you succeed, well I am sure we can give you more time. And, if you don't succeed . . .' he trailed off, the menace thick in his tone.

Nico had no choice but to agree.

* * *

Hobo was packed when Fontaine made her entrance. She swept in; it was just like old times.

Steve Valentine rushed forward to greet her. He looked good. Sexy and smooth. Sammy was doing a great job of circulating, his natural warmth and friendliness appealing to everyone. The new disc jockeys were playing amazing sounds, and even the waiters looked hot in their new black and white uniforms.

Vanessa was already there. 'I love it!' she exclaimed. 'Sweetie, the atmosphere! It all makes Dickies seem rather old and boring.'

'Do me a favour and dance with Paulo,' Fontaine whispered. 'He's boring the pants off me.'

'Is that a bad thing?'

'Oh, didn't I tell you? I've given up sex.'

'You?'

'Yes, darling, me. Don't look so surprised.'

* * *

'How'd it go?' Hal asked.

Nico shrugged. 'Complicated. I shouldn't involve you.'

Hal nodded. 'Suits me.'

'I have to see Fontaine,' Nico said.

'Business or pleasure?'

'Both.'

'You're in luck. It's the Hobo reopening party tonight.'

'Let's go.'

They took a cab over. Nico wondered what the hell he was going to say to her. If it was any other female he would have been able to come up with a whole line of stock phrases. But Fontaine . . . she was different. Life could be very unfair at times.

*   *   *

Fontaine was in her element. All the hard work had been worth it. Everything was zooming along. Hobo was back. She danced with various admirers, and thoroughly revelled in all the attention she was receiving.

Sammy was having a blast too. Three sixteen-year-old groupies and a rock star were his personal guests.

Count Paulo hovered attentively wherever Fontaine went. 'Do take care of him,' she hissed in Vanessa's direction. But Vanessa was busying herself with a short jockey, and his equally boring, rather tall wife.

Leonard invited Fontaine to dance. 'You are coming this weekend?' he asked anxiously as he jigged about in an embarrassing way.

'Of course. I could do with lying about and relaxing.'

Leonard grinned. 'I can hardly imagine *you* relaxing.'

'Oh, I can, you'd be surprised.'

The frantic Black Eyed Peas sound changed to a slow throbbing Mariah. Leonard seized his chance and grabbed her. His hands were hot and sweaty through her dress.

'A little looser, Leonard, I can't breathe.'

'How about lunch one day? Just you and me?'

'What about Vanessa?' she said, edging away from him.

Horny husbands. She wished they would leave her alone.

* * *

Hal had a date with a geriatric widow. He insisted on collecting her and bringing her to the Hobo party.

Nico decided to fill him in on his conversation with Feathers, and Hal whistled and commented, 'Guess it's better than having your legs cut off at the knees!'

Hal really knew how to make a person feel good.

They walked into Hobo, and it was all happening. The place was alive again. Excitement hung heavy in the air. Nico spotted Fontaine immediately. Other women paled beside her; she was a true original. On the crowded dance floor she stood out.

Sammy greeted them effusively, then insisted they join his table near the dance floor and got busy making introductions. Nico caught the name Sandy Roots, and realized that he was sitting with the jockey and his wife.

Hal pointedly tapped Nico on the arm. 'Have you met Vanessa Grant?' he asked.

Nico turned to the plumpish blonde woman and generated full-wattage charm. 'My pleasure, madam.'

Vanessa sparkled. What more could she ask for? A magnetic stare from a very attractive stranger on one side. And her famous but rather short lover on the other.

Fontaine, returning from the dance floor, saw Nico, ignored him, and squeezed between Sandy Roots and the rock star.

Nico leaned across Vanessa. 'Good evening, Mrs Khaled.'

She pretended to notice him for the first time. 'Oh, Nico. How are you?' Her voice was cold, but suddenly her heart was racing like some stupid little teenager.

Count Paulo, sitting opposite her, said, 'Fontaine, we dance now?'

She dismissed him impatiently. 'In a minute, Paulo.'

'How have you been?' Nico enquired.

'Busy,' she replied.

At this point Vanessa got up to dance with Sandy Roots, and just as Count Paulo attempted to sit next to Fontaine, Nico moved up beside her, blocking him.

'You didn't return my calls,' Nico said softly.

'I told you, I've been busy.'

'You had no intention of returning my calls.'

'True.'

He reached out and touched the heart he had sent her. 'But you wear my heart.'

'It's pretty.'

'No thank you?'

'Oh, I'm so sorry. Did I forget to say thank you like a polite little girl?'

'You're still a bitch.'

'And you're still so fucking sure of yourself.'

'Why don't we get out of here? I want to talk to you properly.'

'There's nothing to talk about.'

'In that case we'll make love. We both want to. Then, if you feel like it, we'll talk.'

He stood up, grabbed her firmly by the arm, and propelled her to the door.

She didn't protest. She had no desire to.

Paulo came running after them. 'Fontaine, *bellissima* – what is happening?'

'Go back inside, order a drink, and find someone of your own age to play with, sonny,' Nico said.

'But . . .' Paulo's mouth dropped open while he thought of something to say.

'Goodnight,' said Nico.

And he and Fontaine exited up the stairs.

Chapter Twenty

Dino bided his time for a week. He behaved as he always behaved. He dated a couple of showgirls, wandered around the casino with his usual Tony Curtis smile and reported to his father every day. As far as everyone connected to him could see, Cherry was just a distant memory, a quick brain storm. What had happened was in the past. Dino had been a naughty boy, and Joseph had rapped his knuckles. Now it was all over.

Or was it?

Beneath the ready smile lurked an angry bitter man. What his father had done to him was unforgivable. Joseph had made a public fool of him, he'd annulled his marriage as if he was some crazy teenager.

Dino would never forgive him for that.

* * *

Joseph Fonicetti felt good. Everything taken care of. No loose ends. Even that bastard Nico had been found and warned.

Dino was a fine son. A sensible boy. He'd soon realized the error of his ways. Dumb cunts were not for marrying. They were for humping out of your system.

* * *

Bernie decided there was no way he could marry Susanna again. There were several reasons – the main one being that she would drive him fuckin' nuts! She had a bossy streak that was not to be believed. And nag nag constantly. And Daddy. And Starr, his own kid, a spoilt pain in the ass. But how could he leave with the matter of Nico still unresolved? It was impossible. He knew Susanna, she would go running straight to Carlos and blame everything on him.

He sat in his office and pondered about what to do next. The fifty-thousand dollars was locked securely in his office safe. Unfortunately, he had not yet been able to contact Nico to offer his help.

His secretary walked into the office. She was a long-legged California blonde with lethal teeth and huge silicone breasts. She sat herself on the edge of

214

his desk exhibiting an exciting length of leg. 'Your wife called,' she announced, 'while you were in the john. Wants you to call back right away.'

'She's not my wife, Tina.'

'Ex-wife. So what?'

That was the trouble with secretaries today. No fuckin' respect.

* * *

'I'm flying to L.A. tomorrow morning,' Dino casually informed his father.

'What for?' Joseph asked.

'The usual. Collect personally on a few outstanding markers.'

'Oh, yeah – yeah. Good.'

It was only acceptable to some of the Forum's more famous patrons to have their debts picked up by either Dino or David.

'I thought it was David's turn,' Joseph remarked.

'I'm doing him a favour,' Dino said. 'Mia's not feeling so well, only another six weeks and you'll be a grandpop again.'

Joseph chuckled. David and Mia were doing well for him. A suitable few weeks gap and he would ship in a prospective bride or two for Dino to check out.

'You staying over?' he asked.

'I don't know,' Dino said. 'Maybe, I'll let you know.'

Bright and early the next morning Dino was on a plane.

A car met him at LAX. He knew exactly what he was going to do.

He wasn't nervous any more. He was suitably calm. He was thirty-one years old and perfectly capable of making his own decisions.

Fuck Joseph Fonicetti and all he stood for. He, Dino, was going to be his own man. He wanted Cherry, and goddamnit he was going to have her.

* * *

'Let's go upstairs,' Susanna suggested after dinner.

'I got work to do,' Bernie replied.

'You're becoming a real workaholic,' Susanna complained. 'You can catch up tomorrow.'

Her 'I wanna get laid' look was coming across loud and clear.

'Sure,' he said, realizing suddenly that he was a sex object. *Her* sex object. Something was wrong somewhere.

'So, come on, Bernie. What are you waiting for?' Susanna said, winking slyly and walking ahead of him up the stairs.

* * *

Dino parked outside Cherry's apartment building. He hadn't wanted to phone her, after all, her first reaction might not be exactly friendly. He hadn't dared call her from Vegas – he wouldn't put it past Joseph to have a tap on his phone.

The apartment house was on the seedy side. Peeling paintwork and garbage cans right out front where you could see them. The communal pool had rotten tiles with dilapidated lounging chairs arranged around it.

Dino was used to luxurious surroundings, always had been. He turned up his nose in distaste at the various cooking smells. It was a shame that delectable Cherry had to live in such a sordid place. It stank of failure and survival on the lowest level. Oh well, he would soon be taking her away from it all.

He found her apartment and pressed the buzzer. No answer. So he tried again.

A faded redhead with enormous tits and a sackful of cat droppings emerged from the next-door apartment.

'Hello there,' she said, looking Dino over appreciatively.

'Do you know if anybody's home?' he asked, indicating Cherry's apartment.

'Shouldn't think so. Those little ladies keep themselves *veree* busy. Know what I mean, buster?' She smiled broadly, forgetting the fact that she had not put her two front false teeth in.

Ladies? Dino was surprised that Cherry lived with a roommate, she'd never mentioned it.

'Wanna come in for a coffee, honey?' The redhead leered.

Dino threw her a cold stare.

'Only trying to be neighbourly, dear,' the woman said.

A commotion heralded the arrival of Cherry's roommate. She was a very tall girl, accompanied by two large Alsatian dogs, suitcases, and her porno-movie-star boyfriend, a Mr Universe type.

The redhead shrugged and vanished quickly inside her apartment, cat droppings and all.

'Lookin' for someone?' the girl demanded, while the two Alsatians sniffed around Dino's crotch.

He tried to shove them away.

'Watch it,' Mr Universe porno-movie-star said in a falsetto voice. 'Those dogs are sensitive.'

'Jesus Christ!' the girl exclaimed for no particular reason.

'Is Cherry around?' Dino asked. 'I'm her, uh, friend.'

'I dunno. I've been away.' She turned to her boyfriend. 'For crissakes open the door.'

Mr Universe struggled with the key, and the three of them entered the apartment.

'What the fuck's that God-awful smell?' The girl exclaimed. 'Cherry? You around?' she screeched. 'There's some guy here for you.'

Dino stayed by the door. He didn't like the apartment. He didn't like the roommate. He didn't like the whole set up.

'Shit!' the girl said.

She was certainly no Cherry. More like a tough little hooker.

'You wanna hang around?' she asked unenthusiastically.

'Gotta take a piss,' Mr Universe announced.

A really lovely couple.

'No,' said Dino, 'I'll come back later. Tell Cherry Dino was here, and I'll be back.'

'Suit yourself,' the girl said, shrugging.

'*Sheeiit! Jeez!*' Mr Universe's falsetto tones screamed out. 'Get in here! Get in here quick!'

The girl, Dino and the two Alsatians rushed into the bathroom.

Cherry lay in the tub, naked and quite dead.

* * *

Susanna woke early, fixed a big pitcher of orange juice, and went into her study to work on the design for the wedding invitations.

She hummed softly to herself. It was quite nice

having Bernie around the house again. Only quite, because he was still as neurotic as ever. He picked his nose all over her special lavender sheets. He farted. He sulked a lot. And he was still jealous of Daddy. However, he knew what he was doing in bed. He could do more with his tongue than a whole legion of upstanding pricks.

Susanna giggled to herself.

The phone rang and she picked it up. An incoherent babbling voice was screaming at the other end.

'Who is this?' she demanded.

It was Dino.

* * *

By the time Bernie got up, Dino was already at the house.

Susanna had him comparatively calmed down and coherent.

It must have been shock enough for him to find Cherry's body, but the girl had lain in a bath filled with her own blood for almost a week, which made it even worse.

Cherry had slit her wrists.

After finding her, Dino had run from the apartment, but not before he'd taken a good look. 'Christ, Susy, it was the most horrible sight of my whole life,' he babbled.

Susanna comforted him. She fed him brandy, held him, and stroked his forehead. She and Dino had known each other all their lives. When she was thirteen she'd developed a huge crush on him that had lasted all of six months. They'd made love once when they were teenagers, and ever since that time remained close friends.

'I thought of you immediately,' Dino said. 'I mean you and Bernie knew Cherry.' He broke off and started sobbing again. 'Why'd she do it?'

Susanna shrugged. 'I don't know.'

Bernie couldn't believe the news. Cherry had killed herself. Why? It was such a waste.

He thought of Nico. Knew that his friend would blame himself, and decided not to tell him.

'Dino, you're to stay here,' Susanna insisted. 'You need the rest, I'll call Uncle Joseph.'

Gratefully Dino accepted her hospitality. He had a nagging gut ache and he knew why. Something was bothering him.

Had Cherry taken her own life?

Or had his father arranged it?

It was something he would never know. However, it would certainly be a long while before he went back to the family business.

Chapter Twenty-One

Ricky drove the Rolls. Eyes straight ahead. Face impassive.

He had a feeling that his days were numbered as Mrs Khaled's chauffeur. Ever since their one drunken evening together she had become frostier and frostier. Never once had she mentioned their night of lust. He was beginning to think that maybe it had never happened!

Of course he'd told Polly all about it, thinking that she would enjoy the juicy details. Wrong. Polly had listened, asked questions, pursed her lips, and never allowed him into her bed again.

Women were funny creatures.

They were approaching the driveway of the Grants' country estate. Very impressive. Parked casually outside the front entrance of the mansion were two Ferraris, a Bentley and a Lamborghini.

'We're here, Nico,' Fontaine exclaimed. 'You're going to love the house.'

He held her hand and squeezed it tightly. 'I'm sure I will.'

Fontaine was positively glowing. She even looked different, softer and more relaxed, her biting edginess in abeyance.

Leonard walked out of the mansion to greet them.

He kissed Fontaine while giving Nico a quizzical onceover. 'A little old for you, isn't he?' he murmured discreetly to Fontaine.

'Leonard, I think I'm finally growing up,' Fontaine said, eyes glowing.

'You? How boring. I hope he's rich at least.'

'Naturally. Only that's not the reason I'm with him.'

Leonard nodded knowingly.

Nico, meanwhile, was organizing the suitcases from the trunk of the car.

'Good God!' Leonard exclaimed, noticing all their luggage. 'You're only here for the weekend!'

Fontaine smiled. 'You should know me by now, I can't stand to wear the same outfit twice. Nico's exactly the same. We're soul mates.' She gave Nico a very long and intimate look. 'Aren't we, darling?'

'You *could* put it like that,' he said, eyes locking with hers.

'I *will* put it like that,' she said, smiling.

Their eyes carried on a secret conversation.

Leonard stamped his foot impatiently. 'Shall we go inside?' he suggested.

Fontaine broke the look. 'Wonderful. Who's here?'

'Susan and Sandy Roots, my trainer, Charley Watson, Pearson Crichton-Stuart and a most delightful little Chinese piece.'

'Got your eye on her already, Leonard?' Fontaine mocked.

'Not at all.'

Fontaine suddenly turned her stare to Ricky. 'You can leave the car,' she said brusquely. 'Take the train back to town. I won't be needing you again this weekend.'

Ricky nodded. He'd made a decision. Randy Mrs Khaled could stuff her chauffeur's job. He was quitting.

'Yes, Mrs Khaled.'

Bitch!

* * *

The weekend got off to a good start. Everyone seemed to get along well.

225

Nico watched Sandy Roots carefully. He seemed a nice enough lad, but Nico did not miss the secret glances passing like fire between him and Vanessa at lunch.

After lunch Fontaine decided she wanted to go riding. 'Can we?' she asked Nico.

'I don't feel like it,' he replied. 'You go. Have fun!'

'Come on, old girl,' Leonard said. 'I'll take you. Anyone else want to come?'

'I wish you wouldn't call me "old girl",' Fontaine snapped. 'Nico, are you sure you won't come?'

'I feel like a game or two of backgammon,' Nico said smoothly. 'Anyone interested?'

Pearson Crichton-Stuart piped up with, 'Me, I'm rather good at the game actually.'

Nico winked at Fontaine. 'Then we shall play for stakes, don't you think? Makes the game more interesting.'

Fontaine kissed him on the forehead. 'I'm going to change. I'll see you later.' She whispered in his ear, 'Hustler!'

'You bet!' he replied.

While she was changing she thought about their relationship. Nico was the most exciting, interesting, attractive man she had ever met. After all the boys, here was a real man. And yet he was also mysterious, and she liked that too. She had a horrible feeling that for the first time in her life she was in love. God forbid!

Downstairs Leonard waited for her, and they set off for the stables in his Land-Rover.

'I hope you've bet your all on our horse tomorrow,' Leonard commented. 'In all my years involved with racing I've never seen form like it.'

'Yes, Vanessa told me. I've placed a few substantial bets.'

'That's my girl.'

She didn't want to elaborate and tell him that she had her house and car riding on it. She needed a big win.

* * *

Nico trounced Pearson at backgammon twice, but the man still came back for more.

His tiny Chinese girlfriend, Mai-Ling, watched attentively.

Charley Watson snored, asleep in front of the roaring log fire. Susan Roots had gone out shopping. Nico was the only one who noticed Vanessa and Sandy slip quietly away.

Riding through the wooded grounds was very exhilarating. Fontaine threw her head back and enjoyed the wind tearing through her hair. Terrible for the complexion of course, but so what.

'Let's take a rest,' Leonard shouted.

They dismounted in a clearing, and before Fontaine even had time to think, Leonard was all over her.

She tried to push him off. 'What do you think you're doing?' she asked sharply.

Leonard pulled at her clothes. 'You want it. You can't fool me, this is your scene, you love it.'

Fontaine found herself struggling with him in earnest. 'Leonard. For crissakes stop it!'

'You like it, you want it. I've always fancied you, Fontaine, and don't you deny it. You've always fancied me, too.'

He was tearing viciously at her clothes now.

She couldn't believe what was happening. With a violent kick she managed to throw him off her, but it was too late to stop him having an orgasm.

He rolled on the ground groaning in ecstasy and pain.

Fontaine got up quickly. 'You filthy bastard!' she hissed.

She mounted her horse and rode back to the house, seething with fury.

Nico was still playing backgammon and taking a bundle off the rather chinless Pearson Crichton-Stuart.

'I want to leave,' Fontaine stormed. 'Let's go.'

Nico didn't take his eyes from the board. 'Why?'

Fontaine couldn't think of a reason. The truth was too humiliating.

'I just feel like going home,' she muttered.

'No,' Nico said firmly. 'We're staying for the big race tomorrow, then we'll leave.'

Fontaine had to admit that one of the things she loved about Nico was that he did what he wanted to, not what she told him to.

It made a very acceptable change.

* * *

Dinner that evening was a formal affair. Vanessa had decided it would be fun to dress up.

Nico was in high spirits. He had managed to take over two-thousand pounds off Pearson Crichton-Stuart.

'It's just not done,' Fontaine chided him gently in the privacy of their room before dinner. 'Let the poor fellow win some of it back later.'

Nico laughed. 'You're so English! He wanted to gamble. He lost. That's all there is to it.' For a moment he was tempted to tell her of his gambling debts and everything else. But he curbed the temptation. She would probably be horrified. Worse – she would probably offer to bail him out. And he didn't want her money. Although a couple of her diamond rings would no doubt raise enough to solve all his problems. One lady who would never be caught dead in fake gems was Mrs Khaled.

The opportunity to talk to Sandy Roots in private was not easy. Nico finally cornered him after dinner. He hated what he had to do, but then again, he had no choice. He engaged the young jockey in a this and that conversation about racing. Then he sprung the surprise. At first Sandy pretended not to know what Nico was talking about. Then, at last, he realized that Nico meant business. And of course, in the end, he had to agree. He was just about smart enough to know that his racing career could well be over if Charley Watson wanted it that way. And if Charley Watson found out that he was screwing Vanessa Grant. He would definitely want it that way. No doubt on that score.

'I'll do it,' he finally agreed. 'But I don't know how a lousy bastard like you can sleep at night.'

Nico felt like a lousy bastard. Sandy was right.

Pearson Crichton-Stuart was bugging him for another game of backgammon.

Fontaine gave him a warning look. He blew her a kiss.

'Don't forget to lose,' she mouthed.

'Never!' Nico mouthed back.

'What do you think of Sandy?' Vanessa whispered to Fontaine.

'Sandy?' Fontaine questioned vaguely. 'Oh, you mean the little jockey chap.'

Vanessa rolled her eyes meaningfully. 'Not so little!'

Fontaine didn't catch the drift of what she was trying to tell her at all, she was too busy directing icy stares at Leonard, across the room.

'Leonard's getting fat,' she snapped. 'Why don't you send him away to a health farm?'

'Do you think so?'

'Yes, I do. He's at a dangerous age. True heart attack material.'

'Oh, no!' Vanessa was anxious.

'Oh, yes,' Fontaine replied coldly. 'He's looking positively old.'

'I like Nico,' Vanessa said, changing the subject. 'I've never seen you so . . .'

'Hooked?'

Vanessa giggled. 'It does seem that way.'

'Yes,' Fontaine said, smiling. 'And to tell you the truth, I'm loving every minute of it.'

*   *   *

The day of the big race everyone got up early. It was crisp and cold, but the sun was shining.

Vanessa served a buffet breakfast with the help of three servants.

'This is delicious,' Fontaine exclaimed. 'I haven't had kippers for simply years!'

Nico picked up a copy of *Sporting Life* and started studying the form. Since Garbo would definitely not be winning the big race he may as well check out the other runners.

He found a real outsider. A French horse called Kanga. Twenty-five to one. The odds were right, so he decided to phone Hal and find out the form.

Hal was encouraging. He knew of the horse. It had come second in a race earlier in the season. Since then – nothing. But the early form was promising, and if the weather conditions were right . . .

'I want to place my bankroll on it,' Nico said.

'What bankroll?' Hal said, roaring with laughter.

'I held ten thou back when I paid Feathers. I want you to get on to two or three bookies and place it for me. Wait until just before the race. I want to keep those odds.'

'It's a gamble,' Hal warned.

'Ah,' replied Nico. 'But isn't that what life is all about?'

Chapter Twenty-Two

Bernie was the last to realize what was going on. And when he found out he was the most grateful.

It all started very innocently. Dino moving in with them. Susanna consoling him day and night – sometimes very late into the night. And Susanna suddenly Miss Sweetness and Light. No nagging. No mention of wedding plans. And certainly no scx.

When Bernie thought about it after, he realized what a dumb schmuck he must have seemed to both of them. He almost laughed out loud when he thought of the Dear John scene. It went as follows.

They had dined, the three of them. Then Bernie had gone into his study to work, and Susanna and Dino had stayed in the dining room chatting intently.

An hour later, they had presented themselves to him, hand in hand.

He hadn't even thought twice about their sudden closeness.

'Bernie, we have to talk to you,' Susanna said. 'Make yourself a stiff drink and sit down.'

Christ! Nico! The sons-of-bitches had done something to Nico.

'I don't need to sit down and have a drink,' he said, frowning. 'What the fuck is going on?'

Susanna had come to him then. Comforting hand on his arm, maternal cluck-clucking sounds coming from the lips.

'I knew you'd be upset, Bernie. Only please, please, for all of us, try to understand.'

'Understand *what* for crissakes?' he was roaring with anger.

'Dino and I want to get married,' Susanna said simply.

'What?' He couldn't believe his ears. Or his luck.

'I know it must be hard for you, but we fought it, we really did, and then . . .' She shrugged helplessly. 'We knew we had to tell you.'

Bernie suppressed the desire to laugh out loud.

Susanna and Dino. What a pair! And Joseph and Carlos would be celebrating for weeks – months even.

Bernie forced his face into a suitably miserable expression.

Dino said smoothly, 'I know it's tough, but Jeez – it's hit us both like a ton of bricks.'

A ton of shit more like.

'I'm confused . . .' Bernie managed to mumble.

'Yes. You must be,' said Susanna, her voice becoming more businesslike. 'The thing is, Bernie, I think you should move back into the house you were sharing with Nico.'

Oh, sure. Get rid of him immediately.

'We've discussed everything,' Susanna said. 'And we all know how close you and Nico are.'

She made them sound like a couple of closet queens!

'So,' Dino continued, 'we've decided to allow Nico more time to pay. I've spoken to my father about it and he's agreed. Three months. But that's the limit.'

It was a swop. Bernie had to move out of Susanna's life with no fuss and bother, and Nico would get more time.

'How about six months?' Bernie ventured.

'Forget it,' Dino snapped.

'They're being very fair,' Susanna said, in her new Florence Nightingale voice.

So Bernie had moved out. What an escape!

He phoned Nico in London immediately with the

good news, but the hotel operator informed him that Mr Constantine was away for the weekend and would not be returning until Monday.

Oh, well, the good news would just have to wait.

Chapter Twenty-Three

The racetrack was packed.

Fontaine, wrapped up warmly in a Yves Saint Laurent pant suit, and a three-quarter length red fox jacket, squeezed Nico's arm tightly. 'Isn't this exciting!' she cooed. 'Have you backed Garbo yet?'

He shook his head. He had just placed the three-thousand pounds he'd ended up winning from Pearson Crichton-Stuart with various bookies around the track. And all of it was riding on Kanga to win. Plus the ten-thousand Hal would have placed for him.

'Oh, but you must,' Fontaine insisted. 'It's a sure thing. Cannot lose. And it better not lose either, I have my house and car riding on it.'

'What?' he stared at her in disbelief.

'I didn't want to mention it before, darling, but I

am slightly what they call busted out. So I have risked everything except my jewellery today. I told you it was exciting!'

Nico could not believe what he was hearing. Fontaine broke. Ridiculous!

'Excuse me, my darling,' he said quickly. 'Little business I have to attend to.'

'Don't forget to back Garbo,' she called after him.

Nico rushed through the crowds. He had to find Sandy pronto. For once in his life – well, the first time since Lise-Maria actually – he was putting someone else before himself.

'*Don't be a fool,*' a voice screamed in his head.

He ignored it.

Finding Sandy was no joke. He managed it, and the jockey was duly relieved and grateful to be let off the hook.

Ruefully Nico went through his pockets to see if he had anything left to place on Garbo. Nothing. Every cent he had was riding on a long chance, now a no chance with the favourite once more in the race. On his way back to Fontaine he passed Lynn and Feathers. She ignored him. Feathers signalled, an imperceptible knowing nod. Nico nodded back. There was only one thing for it. After the race, stick with the house party until he could make a fast exit out of town.

By the time Nico got back to Fontaine the big

race was preparing to start. She was as excited as any schoolgirl.

Nico watched her with affection. He would be sorry to leave her, in fact more than sorry.

Garbo shot right up amongst the first three horses surprising no one. Where was Kanga? Who knew? With all those runners it was difficult to tell. Garbo was holding steady. Running beautifully. Taking the jumps in her stride. A magnificent horse totally at one with her jockey.

At the fifteenth jump the crowds went mad – Garbo fell.

'Oh, my God!' Fontaine exclaimed, fanning herself.

Nico put his arms around her. 'It's only a race,' he comforted.

'Only a race! Nico, I had everything on that horse, bloody everything!'

He hugged her. No need for him to skip town now. 'So we'll be broke together,' he comforted.

'You . . . broke?' she said, eyebrows rising.

'I'm afraid so.'

They both started to laugh at the same time. Hugging, kissing, laughing.

'What shall we do?' Fontaine asked.

'We'll be together,' Nico responded. 'Believe me – we'll think of something.'

They stared at each other as if for the first time, totally oblivious to the noise and chaos around them.

'You'll backgammon hustle, and I'll sell my jewellery,' Fontaine joked.

'Never your jewellery,' Nico said sternly. 'Never. I forbid it!'

'You're so macho,' Fontaine sighed. 'I love your macho side.'

'And you're still a bitch.'

'But you like it,' she purred.

'I love it . . . and you.'

' . . . and you.'

'Give me those lips, those luscious beautiful lips.'

They kissed, and Nico didn't even hear them announce Kanga as the winner of the race.

'I will look after you,' he said. 'But you must promise me – no more flirting. No more Italian studs.'

Fontaine smiled. 'And you. No more oozing charm over any woman who passes your way.'

They looked at each other warmly and embraced.

Over Fontaine's shoulder Nico spotted a stunning-looking girl. He eyed her appreciatively.

Over Nico's shoulder Fontaine saw an extremely handsome young man. She looked him up and down with interest.

They drew back, gazed at each other, and burst out laughing. They were quite a pair, and they knew it.

If you enjoyed *The Bitch*, turn the page to find the
first chapter from Jackie Collins' sexy sizzing classic:

The Stud

The Stud is available from Simon & Schuster
as an Ebook and paperback in 2012.

THE STUD

Chapter One

Tony

There is something very exciting about the beginning of the evening – well, the beginning of my evening, usually about ten-thirty, eleven o'clock. Every night at Hobo is like a party – a great party where everyone knows and likes everyone else.

They start coming in slowly. First the ones that want to be sure of a good table, then the watchers. Usually this whole group is stacked neatly out of the way on the wrong side of the room, or if they are really rough, in the back room. We've got a closed membership, but a few manage to find their way in. Then everyone sits around waiting for the swingers, and about twelve-thirty, one o'clock, they start arriving. Golden-haired girls in cowboy outfits, Indian gear, boots, backless topless see-through dresses. The wilder the better. Their escorts varying from the long-haired mob of rock groups to the latest young actors. Elegant young debs in full evening dress, with chinless-wonder escorts. The older society group. The rich Greeks. The even richer Arabs. An odd movie star – an odd M.P. or visiting senator. Anybody famous who's in town. Young writers, dress designers, photographers, models. They all come to look and be looked at, and to see their friends. It's like a building excitement – reaching a breathless climax at around two a.m. when the room is so jammed you couldn't get anyone else in except maybe Frank Sinatra or Mick Jagger.

It seems ridiculous that six months ago they would hand me a couple of quid and wouldn't recognise me if we passed in the street. Now they can't wait to grab hold of me – 'Dahling' – kiss – kiss – kiss – 'Who's here tonight?' Sly grab if the boyfriend or husband isn't looking. 'Please don't give us a lousy table like last time'– affectionate squeeze and promising look. Then husband or boyfriend steps forward – firm handshake, few masculine chummy words, and I hand them over to Franco, swinging head-waiter supreme, who whisks them off to whatever table their position rates. The watchers on one side of the room, the doers on the other. All very neat, the duds with the bread tucked firmly away in the back room.

Yeah, I'm very popular now, everyone wants to know. Funny thing, isn't it? I'm the same guy, talk in the same voice, the clothes are a little more expensive but that's about the only difference. You wouldn't believe it though, the ladies practically fight to climb in the sack with me. You would think I was doing them a big favour, and listen, the way things have been going I think I am!

I tell you it's a great life if you don't weaken.

I suppose you're wondering how this all came about, how a guy like me, Tony Shwartsburg from somewhere near the Elephant and Castle, turned into Tony Blake – man about town, friend of the stars, host at the most 'in' discotheque, Hobo. I have exchanged confidences such as 'Where can we get some pot?' and 'Got any birds?' with some of the most famous in the land. 'Tony can arrange anything' is a well-known catch phrase around town.

Well, to begin with I had the same useless tough life as most of the kids in my neighbourhood – fighting in the back streets, watching in on the fights at home. My parents, Sadie and Sam, were a nice old Jewish couple who hated each other. Sam couldn't care less about me, but to Sadie the sun shone out of my left ear. 'Learn a trade like your cousin Leon,' she would say, 'let the family be proud of you.' I got laid at thirteen, just before I got barmitzvahed. If the family knew they'd sure as old harry be proud of me. It was all good clean fun. The girl, she was a few years older than me, gave me the crabs, and I spent about six months alternately trying to get rid of them and passing them on to any girl who got lucky! Eventually I passed them on to the wrong girl and everyone found out. Sadie had hysterics and Sam patted me on the back and bought me some ointment.

At sixteen I got caught pinching petrol from a car. It was a good racket while it lasted. You hosed it out into a can, and sold it back to the garage where it had probably come from in the first place! Anyway, they shoved me on probation and that was the end of my criminal tendencies.

I got a variety of jobs, delivering papers, sweeping up in a factory, usher in the local cinema – I got fired from that when the manager found me making it with a bird in the back row of the stalls. It was his best usherette and he was screwing her at the same time, so he was a bit choked. Unfortunately I knocked her up and there was a family scandal, but seeing the manager wanted her back, as good usherettes were hard to come by, he paid for her to get unknocked up and everything was all right.

By this time Sadie and Sam were getting a bit fed up with me, and who could blame them? Sam stopped screaming at Sadie and started on me. It was a good job someone thought of Uncle Bernie.

Uncle Bernie was the success of the family. He owned two delicatessens and had sort of cut himself off from the rest of his clan. Anyway Sadie felt that as she was his only sister he owed her a favour, and she dragged me down to his place in Great Portland Street and insisted he gave me a job. He wasn't too thrilled at the prospect, but knowing he wasn't going to get rid of Sadie any other way, he agreed.

He had a daughter, Muriel, a big strapping girl with lots of thick black hair – everywhere – you name a place, Muriel had thick black hair there. She wasn't bad apart from that, a bit sexy looking. Big tits and a thin crooked nose. I suppose I shouldn't have, I mean she was my cousin and all, but one day the opportunity arose, and if the opportunity arises who am I to put it down? Of course Uncle Bernie found out and there ended my career in a delicatessen. It was all too much for Sadie, and even Sam wasn't pleased about it.

Life at the Elephant was becoming a drag anyway, and having got as far as Great Portland Street, I thought why not go a bit further. I got a job as a dish-washer at the Savoy, and a room in Camden Town. Life was great. I entered my twenties a happy man.

I met a girl, Evie, a pretty curly-haired blonde; she was a hostess at a clip joint. She fixed me up with a job as a waiter and I discovered the world of tips. It was great, taught me a lot about people. Taught me the right way to milk a pound from a drunk whose intention was to leave nothing.

I was making twenty quid a week. I branched out to striped Italian suits and pointed shoes, then dated girls with a bit more class, hairdressers, shop assistants and all that group. Not bad, I felt like a king! Visited the Elephant on Sundays, and handed Sadie a fiver. Of course she never took it, she always came out with a speech about how I should save my money, settle down, look for a nice Jewish girl and get married, be like cousin Leon – in my opinion a real schmuck.

I left the clip joint and started as a busboy in a high-class restaurant, not so much bread but a road to better things. And the better things were all around me. The birds that came into the place. Beautiful! Furs, jewellery, expensive smells.

From there I became a waiter in another high-class place and I became involved with Penny, daughter of the owner. Penny was something else. Red hair, she was very neat, small and compact. I suppose I fell in love with her. Couldn't make it, that was probably why. Looking back on it now, I reckon she was undersexed, but at the time it bothered me a lot. She was the first girl that I had wanted and couldn't have.

I don't want to sound conceited, but imagine a taller Tony Curtis with a touch of Michael Caine and Kris Kristofferson.

Anyway Penny and I wanted to get married. Her father of course was furious, but she got round him and since he didn't want his daughter marrying a waiter he opened a new place and put me in charge – sort of a de luxe head-waiter.

It all started there. That's where I first saw Fontaine.

Of course everyone's heard of Fontaine Khaled, she's sort of like a national institution, though not so old – around thirty-five I would say, even now I still don't know the truth.

Fontaine looks very haughty upper-class English. Beautiful, of course, with chiselled cut bones (by nature or cosmetic surgery no one knows), a fine parchment skin, an angular bony body which lends itself to fancy clothes, and long blonde hair worn pulled back.

When I first saw her I couldn't take my eyes off her. Here was a lady. Sounds corny I know, but there was no mistaking the fact. She had been a world famous photographic model, and had retired to marry Benjamin Al Khaled, billionaire. She was always in the papers, jetting here, there and everywhere, showing us around her house in Acapulco, her castle in Spain, her town house in London or penthouse in New York.

I read the columns a lot. In my business it's always good to know who's who, so as soon as she came in I knew it was her. She was with three men and two women all of the same social scene but not in the same class as her. I led them to their table personally, a thing I had stopped doing when I took over the place. I even referred to her by name just to let her know I was around. But she didn't give me a glance. So much for the instant impact of Tony Blake.

There was no Benjamin Al Khaled with her, and I didn't think she was anyone's date, very square the fellows with her, typical no balls types, with loud public school voices.

She was wearing what I thought was a rabbit coat, but later I discovered during a course of intensified education that it was chinchilla. I thought I was pretty hip then, but I didn't even know a Gucci handbag from a Marks & Sparks.

I hovered around the table a lot, but not so much as a look.

I eavesdropped, 'St Moritz is becoming a terrible bore' – 'Did you know Jamie broke his leg in Tibet?' – 'Do you *believe* St Laurent this year?'

Pretty dull snatches of conversation came my way.

The one that paid the bill left a nothing tip.

Two nights later she was back, this time with her husband. He was much older than her. They were with another old guy. She threw me a brief smile on her way in, which startled me, and after that they came in a lot whenever they weren't flying round the world.

Penny was causing me problems. Since her father had promoted me, so to speak, I was having a fair amount of success. Customers liked me, I remembered their names, saw their food was just right, and became casually friendly with some of them. The place developed a good reputation, people were disappointed if I wasn't there. They liked to be greeted by name and made to feel important.

Penny's father realised I was good for the joint and I realised Penny was no good for me. It was not a good situation. She started to get very narky and jealous, accusing me of all sorts of things, which were true. Well, I don't know if she thought I was jerking off or what, but I certainly wasn't getting any action from her. I moved to a small one-roomed flat off the Edgware Road and she caught me there one day with a red-haired croupier – female of course!

What tears and scenes! She even offered me her virginity but, by that time, I didn't even fancy it. So we parted bad friends.

Needless to say it was a matter of time before her father and I also parted company. I had my eyes wide open for another job. By that time I had had the waiter bit, I wanted to move up in the world, progress. The ideal situation would be to get my own little place, but for that one needed bread, and who had any?

I cast my eyes around and one memorable night they met squarely with Fontaine's. It was one of those looks, her cool aquamarine eyes clashed straight on with my moody dark stare (many's the bird who's told me I've got a moody dark stare) and that was it. We both knew something had to give.

She went to the powder-room shortly after and I was waiting when she came out.

'Tony,' she said, she had a deep, very English clipped accent, 'you're wasting yourself here – why don't you drop by and see me tomorrow, I have an idea that maybe you can help me with.' She handed me a small hand-engraved card with her address and added, 'About three o'clock will be fine.'

I nodded dumbly, to tell you the truth I was knocked out by the whole thing.

I must have changed my outfit ten times the next day – was a casual look best or should I go for the slightly formal Italian gear? I finally settled for a pale lilac shirt with a stiff white collar, and a black silk suit.

I arrived half-an-hour early at this knockout pad she had in Belgravia. It was too much! I found out it was an ex-embassy. They even had a swimming pool.

A butler settled me down in what I supposed was the living-room, but it turned out to be a mere waiting-room. It was all expensive with crazy carved furniture and jazzy old pictures on the wall. Some of them were rather sexy – there was one with three birds and one guy that was a bit strong, but just when I was studying it a bit closer Fontaine came in. 'Are you interested in art, Tony?' she asked.

She looked great in a long sort of silk robe and her hair all loose.

Man, I can still remember how nervous I was. This was real class.

'Let's go in the study,' she said. 'Would you care for a drink?'

I asked for a sherry, I figured it was the thing to have.

'You don't look like a sherry man to me,' she said, her eyes cool and amused.

I started to get excited there and then, and in the tight black trousers I was wearing, this was no joke. I approached her warily, she didn't back away, in fact she came towards me. I put my arms around her, she was tall, I could feel her bones through the thin robe. She fastened her arms about my neck and pulled my mouth on to hers.

It was some kiss, she was like a hungry animal pushing and probing with her tongue, biting and sighing. I think I can safely say I gave back as good as I got.

'Let's go upstairs,' she said at last, and added, 'it's all right, Benjamin is away.'

I followed her to a small elevator and we pressed closely together as it started up. She unzipped my trousers and rubbed me with her long talented fingers. Man, I was ready to shoot off there and then!

Suddenly the elevator stopped and she shrugged off her robe.

I stared at her lean body. She had tiny breasts with pale extended nipples. 'Are we there?' I asked foolishly.

'No, but we soon can be,' she replied pulling at my trousers.

The elevator was small, gave you a touch of the claustrophobia, but she managed to get me down to my bare skin.

I must say in all my dealings with birds I've never had one behave like *this*.

'Tony, you come up to all my expectations,' she muttered. 'Sit down, I'll show you how to do it in a lift.'

Oh man! What an experience!

Thinking back I didn't get a chance to do much because she did everything. Of course I rose to the occasion magnificently. I was out of my depth and knew it. I just let her have her way, I wasn't going to blow this set-up.

She dug her nails deep into my back and twisted her long white legs around me. She didn't moan or cry out. She muttered, 'Screw me, you bastard, keep it hard.'

Well, I'd never had any problem doing *that*.

Afterwards she was all calm and businesslike. She stood up and put her robe on. She waited for me to struggle into my clothes, then the elevator took us back to the study.

I was destroyed. I flopped into a chair. She rang a bell, and the butler appeared with tea.

She chatted away in her high-class tinkly voice and who would have thought that half-an-hour earlier she'd been frothing and raving about in the elevator.

'I want to open a discotheque,' she said. 'Something different, something chic, somewhere to go that's fun – something mad and exclusive.'

'Yes?' I was all interest. Here came my big chance.

'You could manage something like that, couldn't you?'

She chatted on about how there was nowhere to go that was chic. 'All these places now are filled with scruffy little nothings – don't you think this town needs something different – somewhere for grown-ups like Paris has, or Rome?'

Her line of chat killed me. Somewhere for grown-ups yet! However I nodded seriously. I was looking for an out from the restaurant – this could be it.

'You start looking for premises, Tony,' she said, 'money's no problem. My husband will finance the whole thing. We'll pay you a good salary and five per cent of the profits. How's that? Of course you'll be running the whole show, does it appeal to you?'

Did it appeal to me? You bet your ass it appealed to me.

She stood up, smoothing her robe down. 'I have to get dressed now. Start looking and keep in touch.' She turned at the door. 'Oh, Tony, in the lift, that was nice, very nice, let's do it again soon.' Then in the same cool voice she added, 'The butler will show you out.'

It was all too much. This was a real cool lady and a raver to boot. I had a feeling I'd fallen in the right direction.

I set to work, started getting up early in the mornings and hanging around the estate agents, saw a lot of lousy joints. I had a feeling for what she wanted (ha ha) and I kept right on looking until I found it. It was a rooftop restaurant that had gone bust – bad neighbourhood everyone said, impossible to park – but baby, you get the right doorman and nowhere's impossible. To me, it was just right. Not too big, not too small. Different because instead of creeping down to some cellar you went up and you had windows and a view. I called Fontaine right away, and she came gliding over with a chauffeur in a Silver Cloud Rolls. She loved it too. We were in business.

We had tea at Fortnums. I hadn't seen her since

the day at her house. She was wearing a silver mink coat and hat, and everyone turned to take another look.

She stared at me with those cool eyes and I knew the look. 'Benjamin's home,' she said, 'but I have another place.'

'Well, let's go,' I said, gulping down dainty tea sandwiches and feeling pretty good.

She dismissed the chauffeur and we took a cab to a small apartment building in Chelsea. It was one room luxury, a big bed covered in white fur, rugs, mirrors everywhere, louvred shutters to remove the daylight and red-tinged lights. A few erotic pictures on the wall, a lot of dirty books in a built-in bookcase next to the bed.

'This is my whore's room,' she said with a small tight smile. I didn't know what to say, I'd never met anyone like her before. She took off her clothes and stretched out on the bed. I fumbled with mine, I mean, well, I was embarrassed!

I finally got them off and started some action. She just lay there very stiff, smiling slightly. Very different from the last time. It was rather exciting really, took me off guard so to speak. I mean, I was expecting it to be like the last time.

It didn't take me long before I was through – wowee! I rolled off her and studied our bodies in the mirrored ceiling.

She said very slowly, 'Tony – how would you like to learn to be a good lover?'

I sat up on one elbow and stared at her. Was she kidding? I mean I was all there you know, I'd never been lacking in *that* department.

As it happens, looking back on it now, I suppose she did teach me a lot. Little tricks she'd picked up in Beirut, Tangier, South America. You name it, she knew it. She was a great teacher, very detailed. I grew to look forward to our little classes more than anything. Of course I was knocking off another bird on the side. Fontaine didn't know about it, but it was useful, gave me a chance to do my homework so I'd be in good shape for Fontaine.

Lana was a stripper, a bit of a scrubber but a knockout when it came to practising my lessons. In fact, she added a few ideas of her own. She had the best pair of knockers around, a big full juicy bird. I mean Fontaine was very classy and all that jazz, but a bit lacking in the tits and ass department. A man likes his steak rare, but he needs his bread and potatoes too.

Life was really good. I left the restaurant and started organising the new place. Interior decorators, waiters to find, members' lists, ordering stock. There were a million and one things to do.

Fontaine chose the name, 'Hobo'. It was good, although Benjamin offered the suggestion of calling it 'Fontaine's'. She said that would be tasteless and vulgar. She was right, she was usually right.

And so eventually we opened. Big party, lots of publicity, all the right people. They all came, they always turn out in bulk for anything free. Fontaine personally supervised the guest list and I think that's what started the whole thing off, her guest list. It was such a wild mixture – from rock groups to movie stars to high society to hookers (international ones of course!). It was great. It all just happened, and within a few weeks 'Hobo' was *the* place and all of a sudden I was *the* person to know.

It's wild really, I still sort of expect the bubble to burst. But here I am, Tony Blake – ex-nothing, ex-waiter, now great host, lover and friend of the stars.

Great me!

About the Author

There have been many imitators, but only Jackie Collins can tell you what really goes on in the fastest lane of all. From Beverly Hills bedrooms to a raunchy prowl along the streets of Hollywood; from glittering rock parties and concerts to stretch limos and the mansions of the power brokers – Jackie Collins chronicles the real truth from the inside looking out.

Jackie Collins has been called a 'raunchy moralist' by the late director Louis Malle and 'Hollywood's own Marcel Proust' by *Vanity Fair* magazine. With over 400 million copies of her books sold in more than 40 countries, and with some twenty-eight *New York Times* bestsellers to her credit, Jackie Collins is one of the world's top-selling novelists. She is known for giving her readers an unrivalled insiders knowledge of Hollywood and the glamorous lives and loves of the rich, famous, and infamous! 'I write about real people in disguise,' she says. 'If anything, my characters are toned down – the truth is much more bizarre.'

Visit Jackie's website www.jackiecollins.com, and follow her on Twitter at JackieJCollins and Facebook at www.facebook.com/jackiecollins

This book and all of **Jackie Collins'** titles are available
as eBooks, or as printed books from your local bookshop
or can be ordered direct from the publisher.

Paperback	ISBN	Price
Goddess of Vengeance	978-1-84983-144-4	£7.99
Poor Little Bitch Girl	978-1-84983-546-6	£7.99
Drop Dead Beautiful	978-1-84983-544-2	£7.99
Lovers & Players	978-1-84983-422-3	£7.99
Hollywood Divorces	978-1-84983-547-3	£7.99
Deadly Embrace	978-1-84983-545-9	£7.99
Lethal Seduction	978-1-84983-421-6	£7.99
The World is Full of Married Men	978-1-84983-617-3	£7.99
The World is Full of Divorced Women	978-1-84983-619-7	£7.99
Sinners	978-1-84983-615-9	£7.99
Hollywood Wives	978-1-84983-625-8	£7.99
Hollywood Husbands	978-1-84983-623-4	£7.99
Hollywood Kids	978-1-84983-621-0	£7.99
Hollywood Wives: The New Generation	978-1-84983-522-0	£7.99
Lady Boss	978-1-84983-627-2	£7.99
Vendetta: Lucky's Revenge	978-1-84983-629-6	£7.99
Dangerous Kiss	978-1-84983-631-9	£7.99

Paperback	ISBN	Price
The Love Killers	978-1-84983-633-3	£7.99
Lovers & Gamblers	978-1-84983-635-7	£7.99
Rock Star	978-1-84983-637-1	£7.99
American Star	978-1-84983-639-5	£7.99
Thrill!	978-1-84983-641-8	£7.99
L.A. Connections	978-1-84983-643-2	£7.99
Chances	978-1-84983-610-4	£7.99
Lucky	978-1-84983-641-2	£7.99
The Stud	978-1-84983-646-3	£7.99
The Bitch	978-1-84983-648-7	£7.99